SET ON YOU

A Second Chance Small Town Novel

KELLY COLLINS

BOOK NOOK PRESS

Dedication

For everyone who loves a cowboy.

Other Books by Kelly Collins

An Aspen Cove Romance Series

One Hundred Reasons

One Hundred Heartbeats

One Hundred Wishes

One Hundred Promises

One Hundred Excuses

One Hundred Christmas Kisses

One Hundred Lifetimes

One Hundred Ways

One Hundred Goodbyes

One Hundred Secrets

One Hundred Regrets

One Hundred Choices

One Hundred Decisions

One Hundred Glances

One Hundred Lessons

One Hundred Mistakes

Cross Creek Novels

Broken Hart

Recipes for Love
A Tablespoon of Temptation
A Pinch of Passion
A Dash of Desire
A Cup of Compassion

The Second Chance Series
Set Free
Set Aside
Set in Stone
Set Up
Set on You
The Second Chance Series Box Set

Holiday Novels
The Trouble with Tinsel
Wrapped around My Heart
Cole for Christmas
Christmas Inn Love
Mistletoe and Millionaires
Up to Snow Good

Wilde Love Series

Betting On Him

Betting On Her

Betting On Us

A Wilde Love Collection

The Boys of Fury Series

Redeeming Ryker

Saving Silas

Delivering Decker

The Boys of Fury Boxset

A Beloved Duet

Still the One

Always the One

Beloved Duet

Small Town Big Love

What If

Imagine That

No Regrets

Small Town Big Love Boxset

Frazier Falls

Rescue Me

Shelter Me

Defend Me

The Frazier Falls Collection

Stand Along Billionaire Novels (Steamy)

Risk Taker

Dream Maker

Making the Grade Series

The Learning Curve

The Dean's List

Honor Roll

Making the Grade Box Set

Chapter 1

Freedom was one step away. I gripped the cold, steel door frame and looked through the window at what could have been. Joe was there—standing —waiting. He had always been my savior, but he no longer belonged to me. I'd given him up the day I almost killed a man.

Officer Ellis' hand hovered over the red button that would release me. "Are you ready?"

Am I? This moment resurrected the memories of every first day of school. Knees shaking. Palms sweating. Heart racing. To navigate was to survive. I'd survived then, and I would survive now.

"One step forward, right?" I looked back at the old man who had been my jailer, mentor, and sometime friend.

Officer Ellis nodded his head. "Yes, Robyn. Move forward, one step at a time. Don't look back." His voice was uncompromising, like a father reprimanding his child. "Don't come back."

I took in a breath of courage and stood tall. At thirty-two, I could do this. "I'm ready." My voice echoed off the lifeless gray walls. I wasn't sure whether I was ready, but it was now or never, and never wasn't an option.

The door buzzed—the lock released—and I was free.

I stumbled through the steel frame and stopped. A memorable scent caught on the wind and pulled me one step at a time down to him. There was safety in familiarity.

My eyes traveled from his brown suede oxfords all the way to the top button of his light blue shirt. The brown hair I'd run my hands through a thousand times hung in messy waves to his collar. He looked good.

"Look at you. Free at last." He stepped forward and put his hands on my shoulders.

Five years without the touch of a man was too long. My heart pounded. But was it truly from the caress of his fingers—or out of the fear of being free?

"It seems like forever."

I hopped off the last step and looked into the warm brown eyes of my ex-fiancé. If things had gone differently, we would have been married and probably on our second or third child. Here he was, still being who he always had been for me —my rescuer.

"It was forever. Can you believe you've been in there for a sixth of your life?" His voice was filled with warmth and regret. "I always thought that sentence was too long for defending yourself."

"I agree, but there seemed to be a disconnect between my truth and Craig Cutter's version of the truth. Putting a man in a wheelchair for life tends to send sympathy to the other side." My voice faded to a hush. "I don't really want to talk about it. It's all in the past, and I've got to think about my future."

He pulled me to a nearby picnic table and sat across from me. Years ago, we would have been thigh to thigh, but that was then. Today was different, although he wasn't looking at me like it was different. He was looking at me in that same possessive way he did from the beginning. The look that said, *You're mine and will always be mine.* But that wedding ring on his finger sang a whole different tune.

"I was thinking of trying to get my job back at Fight for Freedom. You know I always wanted to buy that place."

It was ironic that the martial arts studio I had worked at was all about fighting for freedom, yet my freedom was taken away because I'd fought. I had thought about that night thousands of times. I'd replayed the scenario over and over again. The only alternative wasn't even an alternative. I couldn't let him hurt me, so I fought.

"About that…Sharon sold the dojang. She got too old to run it, and she moved to Florida."

My heart stuttered and stalled. I couldn't swallow. I couldn't breathe. I felt the same as I did the day that judge laid down his gavel and said, *Guilty.*

"Oh, Joe," I said with dazed exasperation. "What am I supposed to do now? That was my fallback plan."

He reached across the worn wooden table and gripped my hand. "You're welcome to stay with me and Tanya. I inherited my grandma's house. There's plenty of room, Tanya isn't expecting our second until November."

The mention of his wife and kids was like a spear through my heart. That was *my* life. I was supposed to live in his grandma's house with my belly large with his child, not some other woman.

"That would never work. What are you going to say? 'Hi honey, I've brought my ex-fiancée to live with us'?"

"Tanya is a good woman. She'd do what's right. She'd do whatever I asked. She might even be able to get a job for you at the supercenter where she used to work."

The idea of living with my ex and his wife seemed like another prison sentence. I refused to be an albatross around his neck, and working at a supercenter was its own particular sort of hell.

I pulled my hand from his and slammed it on the table, lodging a splinter in my palm. "Damn it, I wanted that studio." I picked at the sliver of wood until it was gone, but the spot still stung along with the news of the studio being sold.

"I know you did, but sometimes life has different plans for us." He looked at his watch, and I knew it was time to let him go. In more ways than one.

"I appreciate your offer, but I can't do it."

Every time I'd look at his wife and child, I'd feel something I shouldn't. I'd feel jealousy and regret, and I didn't have time for those emotions.

There were five years of my life to make up, and I needed to start now.

"So what will you do?"

"I'll go with plan B. Can you give me a ride?"

"Anywhere you want to go."

That was my Joe. He was a good man who would always be there if I needed him. I pledged to myself right then never to need him again. He had a wife and family waiting at home, and if I didn't let him go, his obsessive need to rescue me would come between them. He'd always been like that. That's why he was here to pick me up instead of Mickey. He wouldn't have it any other way.

"Let's go."

I stood from the bench and made my way toward his car. Now that my dream was gone, there was only one place in the world that might stand a chance of feeling like home and only one group of people who might be family.

THE CAR IDLED in the parking area of the ranch. I leaned over and gave Joe a hug, but he pulled me in for an awkward kiss on the cheek. I wormed out of the embrace and pulled the half-empty duffle bag he had kept for me all these years from the back seat. It held everything I had in the world. I gave him one last glance before I headed up the walkway toward the big ranch house.

I stood on the top step and took in my surroundings. There was the big house, a barn, and a huge building of some sort, probably the arena Mickey had told me about. In the distance, eight cabins sat side by side, looking like a brochure for summer camp.

This place was different from what I imagined, but it was full of the people who got Mickey through her prison experience. Maybe they could help me, too.

When I got to the front door, I could hear the girls talking. A metal plaque hung from the wood panel that read *It's open, come on in.* Another below it read *Clean the shit from your boots.*

I walked into the main house to find Mickey and the girls feverishly plotting over her upcoming wedding.

"No, I think the tables should be here, and the bar here." Natalie leaned over a piece of paper that had been written on and erased so many times, there were holes in it.

Holly sat back and rubbed her expanding belly, but no one noticed that I'd entered.

"Hey," I said, but they were so caught up in what they were doing, they didn't hear me. Desperate times required desperate measures. At thirty-two, I was physically fit. I could bench press two and a half times my weight and run hurdles better than a woman ten years younger. Not wanting to remain invisible, I took three long strides and hopped onto the center of the table.

"Attention, bitches! Your favorite trouble-maker has arrived!"

Finally, they noticed me, and before I could say another word, I was pulled off the table and forced into the center of a group hug.

"Why didn't you say something?" Mickey pulled me all to herself and squeezed me tight.

"I did, but something must happen to your ears when you plan a wedding. Deaf as a doorknob, the lot of you." I looked at the paper and shook my head. "The biggest dilemma should not be where the gift table goes, ladies. Have I taught you nothing?"

I pulled the page toward me and started writing. On the opposite side of the arena from the door, I wrote *Male Model Auction*. Next to that, I drew a long rectangle and labeled it *Open Bar*.

Megan looked at the makeshift map and

laughed. "Leave it to Raging Robyn to spend two minutes in front of the map and figure it all out."

'Raging Robyn' was what the guards called me because I didn't take shit from anyone. No one touched me or told me anything. Most women were in jail for drugs or petty crimes. A few murdered their lying, cheating husbands, but not one of them had the skill to snap a neck with one move. That particular talent was mine alone. No one bothered me, and they didn't bother my friends either.

Natalie's blue eyes widened. "Are we having a male model auction? I'm not sure Roland will like that."

"Oh, my God, are you all dick whipped?"

The girls looked at each other and nodded. Every single one of them was in love. I was happy for them, but I'd be lying if I said I wasn't a little jealous. Five damn years I'd given up, all because some asshole had wanted to rob the studio. While I sat in prison, everyone else had moved on with their lives.

Mickey grabbed a six-pack of beer from the refrigerator and handed a can to everyone but Holly. She got a bottle of water.

I flipped the metal tab and watched the bubbles threaten to spill, but they rose and fell.

"Here's to family," Mickey said and raised her drink.

We all raised our cans in salute. I took a long draw of the cold beer and relished the tickle of the carbonation as it slid down my throat. I licked my lips, savoring the taste of freedom. Maybe this wasn't going to be as bad as I thought.

Chapter 2

Mickey handed me the key to my cabin and showed me which one it was. Number six. I'd never been a fan of even numbers, but I'd make do with what I had.

"I put you in cabin six. Everyone who stays there gets hooked up or knocked up. With a five-year dry spell and ticking biological clock, I thought you could use a little extra mojo."

"You leave my mojo alone." I walked into the cabin, and she followed.

"Suit yourself, but there's a bunch of single, hungry cowboys on this ranch."

"There's a hungry ex-con here, too. Is there a place I can buy food?" I didn't have much money, but I did have some, enough to fill a refrigerator with yogurt and beer.

"The girls and I got you covered." She pulled the duffle from my hand and tossed it by the brown plush sofa. This place was all right. It had a sofa and two chairs, tables, a television, a bookshelf with books. Nope, not bad at all.

Mickey led me into the kitchen, where stainless steel appliances lined the walls. She opened the refrigerator with enough fanfare to make a game show host proud. It was filled with my favorite things, like yogurt and beer and fresh fruit.

She pulled out a massive cucumber. "I got this just in case you couldn't water that dry spell right away."

"I'm not having sex with a cucumber." I took it from her hand and bit a chunk out of the center, making it useless for the task she had in mind. "I may have been in prison the longest out of all of us, but I never resorted to anything other than my own fingers."

"Suit yourself. But if you change your mind, the girls left you a vibrator and a pack of batteries in the drawer next to your bed. You know, just in case."

"Now, that might be an option if things get desperate." Things were already pretty desperate, but I didn't want to tell Mickey what I wanted more than yogurt and beer was to get laid—and an ice cold cucumber wasn't going to cut it.

She tossed me a yogurt and spoon. "You should have everything you need. Well...almost everything." She walked back into the living room and fell into the sofa.

I took a seat in one of the two side chairs. The cushion hugged my ass as I settled into the best thing I'd sat on in years. "Pretty sweet place you've got for yourself here, Mic." I peeled the foil top from the yogurt and dug in. It was blueberry-flavored with fruit at the bottom. I pulled a round berry from the plastic cup and slid it into my mouth, letting it sit on my tongue. It was sweet and a far cry from the gallons of plain yogurt the prison served with canned peaches.

"I love this place. It's home." She stretched her legs and kicked her feet up on top of the wooden coffee table.

"And you're getting married, too. Looks like you've got everything you've ever wanted. Judging by the baby bump Holly's sporting, I see you're not the only one." I shook my head. "Still, I can't believe you're marrying a cop."

"No one was more surprised than me," she answered. "But once you get to know him, you'll see he has a good heart. His brothers do, too. Just ask Holly and Megan."

"I'd rather not. A girl can only take so much sweetness before she gets a bellyache." I squirmed in my seat. "Look, I don't mean to sound ungrateful or anything like that, because I know how amazing this place has been for all of you, but I'm not sure it's right for me."

Mickey smiled like she knew something I didn't. "They all thought the same at first."

"You're not listening." I sat forward and leaned my elbows on my knees. "I know what home feels like, Mic. I know what the thing I'm missing feels like, and though I can't repay you enough for letting me stay here until I get back on my feet—this just isn't it."

Everything that felt like home to me was gone. Home was climbing into bed with Joe and making love all night long, but he was married with a second kid on the way. Home was teaching and learning at the dojo, but that was now closed. Home was baked cookies and family dinners—all gone.

Mickey rose from the couch. "You think that now because everything feels foreign, but tomorrow it will feel more familiar—the next day, even more. You might even like it here within a week." She crouched to my level and gave me a hug. "This place is magical and seems to have something for everyone." She stood up and placed her hands in the back pockets of her jeans. "I know you, Robyn. You're probably not up for a community dinner, but if you change your mind, there will be burgers and brats at my house at six." Mickey rocked on her boots and turned toward the door. When she got there, she turned around and said, "By the way, we put some things in the closet we thought you might like. Size eight, right?"

I nodded. Leave it to Mickey and the girls to think of everything. "You're too good to me, Mic. I don't deserve you."

"You're right, you don't, but you've got me, so suck it up, buttercup. This is the first day of the rest of your life. Jail moved in slow motion. Real life runs in fast forward. Don't waste any more time." She opened the door and left.

I stood up and took a tour of my temporary home. Back in the kitchen, I picked up the cucumber and ate it as I walked through the cabin. I wanted it gone before I changed my mind about its potential uses.

The first door in the hallway on the right was a bedroom. Connected to it was a bathroom, and through another door in the bathroom was a second bedroom.

They called this configuration a Jack and Jill. Who knew why? The old nursery rhyme made them both sound like idiots. Maybe that was it. If they put a bathroom between them, they might figure out how to get there without breaking a crown or tumbling after the other.

I analyzed my thoughts and realized that sometime in the past few months, as I served out my sentence alone, I had turned bitter. That was the first thing I had to change. I looked as good wearing bitter as I did wearing pea green. Neither was my thing.

The best thing for me was to sleep it off. A good night's sleep was always good for gaining perspective. I had to practice what I preached. Martial arts taught me to be strong, resilient, patient, thoughtful. Yep, I needed sleep so I could get my head into the right place.

I WOKE EARLY the next morning and relished the fact that I could walk to breakfast barefooted. It took me a few minutes to figure out the coffee pot, but once I did, I was in heaven.

The smell of dark roast filled the air. Back in prison, the only time I got dark roast was when the coffee sat in the pot all day. It turned into mud when it sat too long, but there was that perfect moment before it transformed, and that was four o'clock.

I took my coffee to the front porch and sat on the swing. It wasn't silent here like I'd thought it would be. The metal chain of the swing creaked while I moved back and forth. Horses neighed in the distance. Voices carried on the slight breeze.

I took a deep breath and looked around. I regretted being so harsh with Mickey last night, but I'd told her the truth. I still hoped coming here would fill some gap in me, but I also knew it wouldn't. This wasn't where I belonged. At least not for the long haul. Still, while I was here, I might as well make myself useful. *Burden* wasn't another word I wanted to add to my resume.

I went back into the cabin and started my day with a shower and change of clothes. Once finished, I walked outside to explore the ranch.

The first man I came across was coaxing a horse into the barn. I hurried over to introduce myself and found him standing to the side of the horse, who was mounting a fake mare. The horse's damn dick was over a foot long, and the man was placing a tube over it, but it wasn't going well for him.

He looked up at me and said, "I don't think I'm his type. You want to give it a go?"

I took a step back. "Not unless he's prepared to buy me dinner first."

"You must be Robyn." He smiled. "I like you. You've got spunk." He slid the tube over the massive cock, but the horse's movement sent it flying across the barn. "Welcome to the ranch. I'm Keagan."

"Nice to meet you, Keagan." I thought about shaking his hand, but it was recently touching a horse dick, so I opted out. "Just passing through. I'm here for the wedding, maybe a little longer. But I'm not staying."

"Forgive me for being skeptical, and I don't mean to call you a liar, but you're a liar." He picked up the tube and approached the horse with the twenty-inch dick. "I've definitely heard that before. There's something about this place and you girls that just sort of fits together."

"Nice try. I mean, it has some appeal." I looked at the rigid penis Keagan was covering with a tube. "I prefer my men to walk on two legs and shower, but he's got nice equipment. Is it normal to be so big?"

Keagan laughed. "They come in all sizes and shapes." He nodded toward the table, where a bag labeled 'Diesel Semen Sample' lay. "Can you hand me that biomedical bag?" I picked it up and walked over to where Keagan held the tube to the horse as he pumped against the fake mare.

"Hold this." He took my hand and pressed it to the container. It shook and shuddered as the horse rutted into it with such force, it was hard to maintain a solid grasp.

"Why can't you attach it to this thing?" I pointed to the wooden horse covered in faux fur that had a tail standing straight up.

"Diesel likes a helping hand. He never gets too wild. You're safe."

I couldn't believe I was standing here giving a horse a hand job. Horses were just like men, apparently. They'd fuck anything to get off. He began to grunt and groan, so I turned my head, not wanting to see him reach his completion. My hand shook, and then the container got warm.

"Gross."

"Look at that," Keagan said after taking the sample tube from me. "I guess you're his type after all."

"Well, the horse has excellent taste."

Keagan bagged the sample and put it in his

back pocket before he unharnessed the horse. "Stay here. I'll be right back."

Ignoring his directions, I followed him and the horse out of the barn. Keagan turned left to the stables, whereas I looked right and gazed out to the open meadow. In the distance, a young horse looked to be tangled in the fence.

I rushed to its rescue. The poor thing had yanked and pulled so much, its head hung exhausted between wires of the fence. Afraid I'd witness an accidental hanging of a poor little pony, I charged forward and pushed the butt of the horse with all my might. It popped through to the other side and took off running. That's when I realized I'd made a big mistake. The horse had been escaping, and I was now an accomplice in its crime.

If I'd done that in prison, I'd have increased my sentence by ten years. What would happen to me here?

Not willing to find out, I slipped through the fence and chased after it. If I could just get it back on the other side before anyone noticed, I'd be golden.

As fast as my sneakers could take me, I ran in its direction. I was gaining on the little thing when I tripped over a boulder hidden in the tall grass and tumbled down a hill. When I came to a stop, I was staring at the hoofs of a larger horse. I looked up slowly to see a cowboy glaring down at me. His brows pulled into an affronted frown. His expression was tight and strained.

"I don't think you're supposed to be out here."

Chapter 3

"I'm fine, by the way. Thanks for asking," I said as I stood and brushed the grass and dirt from my jeans. He loomed over me like impending doom. Like a loose virus or swarm of bees ready to attack. His blue eyes turned flat like worn gray concrete.

"I don't usually ask trespassers how they're feeling," he responded, "though perhaps I should start." The horse began to pound its hoof, and I stepped back. "Maybe I'll start asking thieves if they'd like some tea while they steal my things." The horse snorted.

I was prepared to defend myself against people, but I had no idea how to deal with an angry horse. Was I supposed to fall to the ground and play dead? Were they the type of animal that didn't give chase, and therefore I was better running for my life?

But I refused to be intimidated by a horse or man and took a step forward. "I'm not a thief or trespasser." I dug the rubber soles of my sneakers into the grass and stood my ground. "I was just trying to—"

"To steal a colt. I can see that. Now there's only the question of what to do with you. If you tried this shit on my ranch, I'd have the police out here in two shakes of a lamb's tail."

"Good luck." I crossed my arms over my chest. Damn me for having big breasts. Instead of being buried under my arms, my boobs squeezed over the tops of them.

"I don't need luck, sweetheart." He let the reins loose, and the horse lowered its head to nibble at the grass.

"Something tells me the owner of this particular ranch isn't going to be so quick to believe your story."

"You might be surprised," he said. "She's soon to be my sister-in-law."

"Oh, my God. You're a McKinley?" Just my luck to run into one of them and make him angry. Without bad luck, I had no luck. I stepped to his side and offered my hand. "I'm Robyn. I'm a friend of Mickey's."

"I'm Keanan, the oldest McKinley." His voice was gruff, and his eyes shimmered with the intensity of his irritation. In fact, he came off as practically disgusted by me. "You're one of her jailbirds."

"I'm not a jailbird. I did my time, and I'm moving on. Don't tell me you never made a mistake." I looked beyond him in the direction the colt ran. "You let the stupid colt get away."

He shook his head at me. "Don't worry about the colt." He pulled the reins, and the horse grunted. "I doubt you're qualified to handle it anyway, or anything other than printing up a license plate for that matter." He pulled the horse left and galloped away, leaving me in its dust.

I turned and walked toward the ranch. Yep, I was right. This place would never be my home.

By the time I got back to the main property, everyone was in full ranch mode. The hands were moving horses in and out of the stables. In a paddock was another McKinley. They were all tall and dark, but their approachability seemed to be tied to their expressions. Keagan was friendly and appeared angelic compared with Keanan, who was Satan personified. This third McKinley wore a serious expression as he worked with the horse. He must be Megan's beau, Killian, the ranch's official trainer.

As if he could hear my thoughts, he raised his head and nodded in my direction. I reciprocated the gesture with a smile. At least he wasn't ready to lynch me on sight like the oldest McKinley.

Rather than push my luck, I went back to my cabin to catch up on five years of television.

NATALIE STOPPED by after work and asked for my help in preparing dinner. This community living thing might be fine for others, but I wasn't sure it was good for me. I'd done five years of community living, and that had been enough. However, even after my McKinley encounter this morning, I was sticking with yesterday's decision to embrace the time I was here. These women were my family, and I'd do what I could to help out and be useful.

While I peeled potatoes, my mind kept going back to Keanan. What an arrogant asshole he was to think I was less than him. The way he judged me was unfair. It was hard to believe he was related to Keagan, who was so nice.

Hopefully, the man Mickey has decided to spend the rest of her life with is more like the younger McKinley, I thought.

Natalie seemed the perfect person to ask about the men who lived at the ranch. She was the odd girl out, in a way, because her veterinarian lover wasn't a McKinley. So, I went for it.

"What do you know about Keanan McKinley?"

"Not much. He's quiet," she answered. "From what the boys say, he's kind of a stick in the mud, always working. You know what they say about repressed guys, though." She winked. "They're animals in the sack."

I dropped a tater into the sink. "Don't make me sick all over this food." Keanan McKinley was good for one thing only, and that was to ruin my day. "Out of all the girls, I think I'm most surprised by you. I never took you to be a farm girl." I found a rhythm with the peeler and managed to build a mountain of dirt brown potato skins in front of me.

"I'm not, but I found something here I never could anywhere else. I found Roland, and I found myself." She looked down at the dog at her feet. "And I found Pepper." Lying next to the dog was another mutt that belonged to Mickey. She'd named him Buddy. Not the most unique name, but the two dogs seemed happy together. "Pepper is Buddy's dad. So you see, we are a big family here. That's something I never had until I embraced the ranch."

Natalie shucked the corn. Seeing her enjoy manual labor gave me a giggle. Even in prison, she'd found a way to avoid anything that resembled work.

"You really have changed."

"What can I say? I'm a different person now." She nudged me. "A happier person."

Once the prep was finished, we set the big farm table in Mickey's house. With people arriving for Mickey's wedding, the girls explained, someone volunteered to cook each night. Tonight was Natalie's turn, tomorrow would be Megan's, the next night was Holly's. And then there was silence…which I imagined meant *I* would be up after that. Not looking forward to it, but that's what a family did.

DINNER WAS LOUD AND LIVELY. I watched my friends interact with each other like a family. And they were. They were all connected to a McKinley, except for Natalie, but Roland was an unofficial McKinley. The McKinleys seemed to be the glue that held it all together.

Kerrick and Mickey were the perfect match, as were Killian and Megan, Holly and Keagan, and Natalie and Roland. Even the dogs paired up nicely. I couldn't help feeling like the odd woman out. Not only did these women have a new setup and rhythm here, so did their men. It was one big, happy family, and although the introductions and niceties told me I was more than welcome to join in, I still felt like a square peg trying to fit into a round hole.

Just as dinner ended, Keanan came in and grabbed some stuff from the pantry.

"Come sit with us," Mickey offered.

I remained silent. No matter whether he stayed or left, I'd pretend he wasn't here either way.

He looked around the table and shook his head. "I'll pass. There's work to be done."

"Okay, well, I can put a plate together for you so it's ready when you get hungry." Mickey's face fell, and I wanted to stand up and sidekick the asshole for hurting her feelings. It was obvious winning him over was important to her.

"You really should be out checking the fences.

One of your colts almost got away today. It would have if not for me." Keanan glared at me with accusatory eyes. He might as well have thrown a rope over the tree for a lynching.

"Keanan, this isn't your ranch. You don't get to make demands here." Kerrick's stern voice was a warning to his brother to lay off. "You're a guest here. Act like one."

Keanan shrugged and walked away.

"Don't mind him. He never was good with people, and he hasn't really been himself for a couple of years now."

That statement made me curious. What had happened to Keanan a few years ago? I wanted to ask, but Keagan shut his brother up before I could press for more information.

Later that night, after I watched two seasons of *The Vampire Diaries* and drank three cups of coffee, I went to bed. I wasn't sure whether it was the coffee or lying in a comfortable bed for the first time in years, but I couldn't sleep. Nothing felt quite right.

I climbed out of bed and pulled on some clothes. Maybe some fresh air would help. I stepped out onto my front porch and turned my face into the gentle evening breeze. It carried the scent of grass and horse shit.

I walked behind the cabins, past the staff stables into the field where I'd walked that morning. In the distance, I could see the colt back at the fence, pushing his head through the weak spot again.

"Will you ever learn?" I said to no one but myself while I made my way to lend a hand to the rogue pony.

On the way, I caught some movement out of the corner of my eye. In the distance, the silhouette of a man was pulling off his shirt. I looked at the pony and then back to him. He was certainly more interesting than the horse's ass up ahead.

I knelt in the tall grass and watched him for a moment. He dropped his pants and turned, as if he sensed my presence. I gasped. It was Keanan, and he was hung like Keagan's prize stallion, Diesel. Maybe not twenty inches, but more inches than I'd ever seen on a man.

The sight of him mesmerized me. It had been years since I'd seen a naked man, and I wondered whether maybe he was merely a mirage. That thought ended when he reached down and stroked his length. A powerful surge of heat raced through me and settled into an ache between my legs.

As his eyes skirted the field, I hunkered lower,

hoping not to be seen. As if he sensed my presence, he turned his back and gave me a full view of his glorious ass. Even from this distance, I could tell those round globes were as solid as granite. Moments later, he disappeared with a splash into the watering hole. Evidently, he didn't see me.

Feeling like a stalker, I turned toward the colt, who whinnied his distress. I slunk out of the grass and crawled to the fence, where I pulled him free and guided him back to the field he was supposed to be in. If this horse didn't have a name, he needed to be called "Houdini."

I glanced over my shoulder at the watering hole. Thankfully, no naked cowboys were visible. I seized my chance to get the horse back in place, sight unseen.

Chapter 4

Well past eight, I headed to Mickey's to see whether I could make myself useful. I found her sitting at the big table in her kitchen. I grabbed the bowl of crockpot oatmeal she offered and took a seat beside her.

"I'm so glad you're here. I was hoping you could come to town with me. I have to get things finalized for the wedding."

"Sure."

Going to town sounded like a good plan. It got me off the ranch and away from the man who'd haunted my dreams last night. I'd gone as far as putting the batteries in the vibrator before talking some sense into myself. That man didn't deserve to be on the breath of my orgasm. And since I couldn't think of anyone else to masturbate to, I'd tossed the silicone dick back into the drawer and gone to sleep.

"Is there much of a town?"

"There's more to see out here than you would think," Mickey said as Keanan entered the room. My eyes saw a fully clothed cowboy, but my mind went back to what he looked like in the light of the moon—and nothing else. Heat rushed up my neck to my cheeks.

Thankfully, Keanan appeared to be preoccupied with filling a bowl full of oatmeal.

I hurried through my breakfast and got up to bus my bowl. As soon as I got close to Keanan, he leaned over and whispered, "Get a good look last night?"

I dropped my bowl into the sink, causing a loud clatter. "Shit." *He saw me!*

"You okay?" Mickey asked.

"Yes," I croaked out.

I looked toward a relaxed Keanan, who leaned against the counter, eating his oatmeal as if he hadn't outed me. Somehow, I managed to get the bowl rinsed and into the dishwasher without further disaster.

Once finished, I headed straight for the door. "Are we leaving soon?" I called over my shoulder.

I prayed she would say yes because I needed to get as far away from that man as possible. If I stayed, there were two possible outcomes. I'd either kill him and end up back in prison, or I'd fuck him and want to kill myself for making such a shit choice.

"I'll swing by in thirty minutes to get you."

"I'll be ready." I took off out the door like a mouse being chased by a cat. This particular cat was dark-haired, blue-eyed, and as tall and thick as an oak tree. He was one freaking big animal.

Even from across the field, I could feel his eyes on me, and I swore I heard him laugh.

Thirty minutes later, Mickey honked the horn of her old pickup. I dashed from the protection of my cabin to the safety of her truck. Thankfully, Keanan wasn't anywhere in-between. I would have plowed him straight under rather than face him.

Once inside, I tried to get my mind off the cantankerous cowboy. "I can't believe you're getting married."

Mickey ground her truck into first gear, and it sputtered forward. "I know. It's surreal, but it's so real."

I'd spent some time last night at dinner with Kerrick, and I had to admit, he was a good guy despite his chosen profession. "I like him, Mic. He's perfect for you."

We drove under the Second Chance Ranch sign, and I smiled. She really had turned this place into something more. After listening to everyone's stories last night, I realized it wasn't just a place for her ex-convict friends; she'd changed the lives of Kerrick, Keagan, Killian, and Roland, too.

"We're perfect for each other. Although I couldn't stand him when I first met him. He was easy on the eyes, but he grated on my nerves like fingernails on a chalkboard."

"Really? Why?"

The tick of the turn signal filled the air. "The McKinley men think they rule the world. All of them have been retrained except for one." She shook her head. "I can't figure Keanan out. It's not like he's mean. He's simply unfriendly." She took a right-hand turn and merged onto the highway toward town.

Maybe that was another issue with Keanan. Maybe this ranch symbolized the loss of his family. Whereas he was used to being in charge, he couldn't make his siblings conform on someone else's ranch.

I pretended not to have noticed. "I wouldn't

know. I've had little exposure to him. I have wondered why he's here so early with the wedding still more than a week away."

"There's a big horse auction. It's one of the biggest in the United States. We were going to host one that specialized in quarter horses so Keagan and Killian could show off what they've accomplished here, but with the junior rodeo we held last month and the wedding, we had too much on our plate."

"That makes sense. Now tell me about this wedding."

Mickey bubbled with excitement about the wedding. She described how they were going to ride out to the meadow that sat above her family's cemetery because she wanted her dad to be there. They would be married on horseback, with the non-riders being driven by carriage. By the time she was finished, I was as excited as she was. Happiness was obviously contagious.

A few miles later, Mickey pulled in front of a wedding dress store, which didn't surprise me. Weddings needed dresses, and Mickey needed hers. What did surprise me was that she'd brought me here for a last-minute fitting for a bridesmaid dress. I'd never dreamed there would be enough time to get me a dress. I assumed I'd be standing on the outskirts looking in, but that wouldn't be the case. Mickey wanted me in her wedding and had made sure it would be possible, and that meant the world to me.

Mickey thumbed through the racks while we waited for the saleswoman. She pulled a gown from the sale rack and tossed it to me. "Try this on."

"What? No. I'm not getting married."

Marriage was so far out of my lane at this point. My chances were better for winning the lotto than finding the right man. Even Joe had seemed a bit creepy when he picked me up. He talked about his wife and kid, but he ate me up with his eyes like I was his favorite chocolate pudding.

She dropped to her knees and begged. "Please?"

How could I refuse? I checked the size and rushed toward the dressing room. The faster I got this on, the faster I could get it off. I had no idea what kind of gown this would be called, but it hugged every curve I had. My breasts spilled from the beaded top, but not in a way that made it seem too small or my boobs too big. It was as if the dress was custom fit for my body.

I took a deep breath and said, "I'm coming out."

"We're ready," Mickey exclaimed. I thought she meant she and the saleswoman were ready, but when I walked out of the dressing room, I nearly fell over. Standing next to Mickey was Keanan.

My arms flew across my chest to cover the girls, but by his wicked grin, I knew I was too late to cover anything. Not my boobs, and not my shock at his presence.

"What are you doing here?"

"I left my purse at home, and Kerrick volunteered Keanan to bring it to me. Wasn't it nice he did?"

We both looked at him. *Nice* didn't seem part of his repertoire. Then he did something equally out of character. He smiled.

"You sure do clean up nice for a criminal," he said before he turned around and left.

Mickey watched him walk away, with a look of confusion on her face. "That man is a conundrum." But when she turned to me, the look changed to elation. "You look amazing in that. It was my first choice for a dress, but I didn't have enough booty to fill it out. Your ass looks perfect."

The store clerk entered. "Oh, my God, that fits you like it was custom made for your body. Are you getting married, too?"

"No!" I nearly screamed. "I'm not."

"Too bad. That dress is a steal." She pulled a pink dress from the plastic bag she was holding and handed it to me. "I get it; always the brides-maid and never the bride. I feel your pain."

I rushed into the dressing room. This girl had no idea how much pain I'd endured. How much I'd given up. I took one last look at the perfect dress before I let it slip from my body. Once I had the other dress on, I walked back out to show Mickey.

"It's perfect, too. I almost hate you for that."

The salesperson circled me, pulling and pinching the fabric. "I think it's a go as is. You're a perfect size eight with a Hollywood hourglass figure."

Mickey and the saleswoman looked at me and said in unison, "We hate you." Then Mickey walked to me and hugged me tightly.

"But I love you, too." That was the interesting thing about emotions. There was always a fine line between love and hate. "We'll take it."

"How about lunch?" I asked.

Mickey's eyes lit up. She recited several

nearby restaurants until her phone rang. I heard an exasperated, "Really? Well, shit." She hung up and gave me a pouty look.

"The caterers are there to drop off the tables and chairs. They're days early." She let out a low-pitched growl. "Can I have a rain check?"

"Sure, no problem. Do you mind if I hang out in town for a bit?"

The last thing I wanted to do was go back to the ranch. I couldn't get Keanan off my mind. The way he looked in the water. The way he looked at me when he saw me in that dress. I had to put some distance between him and me.

"No, I don't mind. How will you get home?"

Home was still an odd word for me; despite what Mickey had promised, nothing about that place felt like home—yet.

"I'll catch a cab. I need to turn on my phone and do some banking stuff. You know, that stuff you have to do when you're not in prison."

"I got ya." She gave me a thoughtful look. "Everything is going to be okay, Robyn. It takes a few days to adjust."

I took a deep breath. The air smelled like exhaust and an approaching storm. I always loved the smell of fresh rain. I looked up into the sky, expecting to see the buildup of clouds, but only a wisp moved like a brush stroke against the blue. Yep, Mickey was right. It would be okay; I just needed a few days to figure it all out.

Mickey went right, and I turned left toward the phone store.

Miraculously, my old number was still available. Once I upgraded my phone and visited the bank, I headed to a bar. There were two choices nearby. One was called Rage, and the other was called Spurs. I walked into Rage hoping to avoid any thoughts of naked, well-hung cowboys.

Chapter 5

I sank into a corner booth and looked around. My eyes shifted directly to the man at the end of the bar. Of course he was here. That was my luck —all bad.

I watched him order a beer. The waitress leaned over and practically poured her tits into his hands. A thread of jealousy laced through my gut, even though I had no reason to be envious. Keanan McKinley was not my type. I considered going somewhere else, but I sort of wanted to stay and watch him in spite of the fact that I kind of hated him.

Another woman approached him, but he turned the other way, giving her the brush-off. He obviously had standards beyond most men's basic criteria for a woman: breathing and willing.

So engrossed in trying to figure out Keanan, I barely noticed the man who slid into the booth next to me.

"Hey, darlin'." Sour whiskey wafted across the booth and nearly gagged me.

I was startled by his presence, but I'd been trained not to show it. My eyes scanned the room and found proof that there were plenty of empty seats available.

"I'm not looking for company." I nodded toward some empty booths on the other side of the room. "Find yourself another place."

"I think I'll stay right here. I like the view." His beady little eyes raked over my chest. Subtlety wasn't his strength.

"I'm not interested."

I exited the booth and walked away. I didn't need any trouble, and this guy carried its stench like rotting roadkill. With Keanan swiveled in his stool and facing the front door, I rushed toward the back hallway, hoping he wouldn't see me exit. I was almost out the back door when I heard the creepy guy's voice behind me.

"You don't have to be interested. You just have to be quiet."

My stomach coiled, and I felt bile rise in my throat. The cold outside air reached me at the same time as he did. He grabbed my arm and pulled me toward him.

"Come on, darlin', show me a little respect."

Instincts kicked in. There was a good chance I'd be back in prison before nightfall, but I wasn't going to let anyone hurt me the way I'd been hurt before. No man would do that to me again.

"I'm warning you. Let me go, or you'll regret it." He had his warning.

"I like a little fight in my women."

"Wish granted, asshole."

I stomped on the top of his foot, and when he doubled over, I shoved my elbow into his nose. The crack echoed through the alleyway.

"You fucking bitch."

He swiped the back of his hand across his bloody nose. To say he saw red was an understatement. His face gushed like a geyser, but that didn't stop the asshole from pulling a knife from his pocket.

"You'll pay for that."

He held the knife out in an attack position. *What the hell am I supposed to do now?* I didn't want to die, but I also didn't want to kill him and spend the rest of my life in prison.

"Just leave. I don't want to hurt you, but I will."

"You'll hurt me?" He lunged forward, swiping the knife through the air. "Sweetheart, you don't bring fists to a knife fight. You got in a lucky hit, but it won't happen again."

This was escalating out of control. I was trained to disarm a man, but I didn't want to break the asshole's arm. He could walk away with a broken nose; a broken arm was a scenario that would require more explaining. The last thing I wanted was trouble, but it always seemed to find me.

As I got ready to spin, deflect, and snap the asshole's arm, there was movement in the doorway. It was Keanan, and he was on the guy like flies on shit before I could say another word or think another thought.

One punch from Keanan's meaty fist, and he dropped like a stone.

"You okay?" he asked, but before I could answer, I heard the sirens in the distance. This wasn't going to end well.

Several minutes later, the police were with us in the alleyway. The perpetrator, Ted, sat against the wall while Keanan and I gave an account of what happened. Kerrick rounded the corner minutes later. He headed straight for his big brother.

I leaned against the opposite wall and listened as Tipsy Ted gave his statement about how I seduced him and coaxed him into the alley so I could rob him.

"You're a damn liar!" I screamed with enough fire in my voice to melt metal. "He's lying, and he's going to get me in trouble." All I could think about was how I was going to explain this to my parole officer on our first visit. Would my probation be rescinded because of a lying jerk who wanted a piece of ass?

Kerrick moved in front of me. "Robyn, I'll talk to your PO, but you have to calm down. Witness accounts—" he looked at his brother "—prove you've done nothing wrong."

"Okay." I held out my shaking hands and clenched them into fists, still prepared for an attack. "I just want to go back to the ranch." My voice didn't belong to me. It was the voice of a frightened woman. Someone I didn't recognize.

"If she's free to go, I'll take her back," Keanan said.

Kerrick went back to talk to the officers. I watched them go back and forth. I heard him say, "Look at her, she weighs a hundred and twenty pounds wet. This piece of shit has to weigh at least two-fifty. He's lying."

Once the officers explained to Ted that I could also press charges for attempted rape and kidnapping, he thanked the officers for their time and limped out of the alley.

Kerrick and Keanan exchanged a few words, and then I was alone with the one man I was trying to avoid.

Keanan opened and closed the fist of his right hand. It was then I noticed his bloody knuckles.

"Oh, my God, are you okay?" I brushed my fingers over his abraded skin.

"It's nothing but a scratch. I'll live. What about you?" He turned and looked at me. "Are you okay?" Warmth and concern filled his eyes. It was the first time I'd really had a good look at them. They were the bluest of blue, with tiny specks of light brown around the iris.

"Just shaken up. I'll be better as soon as we get out of this alley."

"Let's get you better, then." Keanan placed his hand on my lower back and guided me to his truck—a big black truck as intimidating as the man who drove it.

I was confused at his sudden personality change. Why was he being so kind and offering his help?

He opened the door, and I jumped into the

cab of the truck, just happy to distance myself from the trouble in the alleyway. "Buckle up. I'd hate to save you in an alley and lose you in a car accident."

In seconds, he rounded the truck and hopped into the driver's side and we were on our way.

Twenty minutes of silence later, he pulled into the ranch, but rather than stop at my cabin, he kept driving.

"Where are you going?"

"You wanted a drink before. That's why you went to the bar in the first place, right? I figured you need one now more than ever."

He drove me out to a field on the far end of the ranch and stopped. "Come on out."

I slid from the front seat to the ground and followed him to the bed of the truck. He went to lift me up, but I pushed him away. I was used to helping myself. He looked at me curiously and then took a seat next to me.

"I thought we were going to get a drink." I looked over the long expanse of land dotted with livestock, yucca plants, and small pools of water and thought about last night and how wonderful Keanan looked by the water.

He leaned back and pulled a six-pack of beer

from the cooler. "This is a BYOB location." He popped the tops of two cans and handed me one.

"It's beautiful out here." The colors were so vibrant. Against the yellow grass and purple wildflowers, the horizon glowed orange in the distance like the plains were on fire. The sky was blue with wisps of clouds floating throughout. Far above it was broken by a jet's contrail. "Is it like this where you live?"

"Yes, but it's better in Wyoming because that's home for me. It's where I belong. It's where I thought I'd raise a family."

"Thought?" I turned to look at him. Finally, he was going to share something about himself.

"Damn it!" Keanan jumped off the truck bed and stomped toward a speck of brown in the distance.

"What's wrong?"

"That damn colt is loose again." He downed the rest of his beer and tossed his can in the back. He reached into the back seat and grabbed a length of rope.

I hopped off the bed of the truck and raced after him. "Why do you think he keeps breaking out?"

Keanan walked while I jogged to keep up.

"Maybe he's looking for a place that feels like home."

"I can empathize." It had been a long time since anything felt like home for me.

"Not me," he said. "I've always known where I belonged."

When we got to the colt, he looked like he was ready to bolt, but Keanan used a soft voice and soft touch that made me want to let him harness me and take me back to the ranch. There was something sexy about a hard man with a soft side.

Once he had the rope around the colt's neck, we walked him back to the ranch. "Wasn't it confusing growing up?"

"What are you talking about?"

"Sorry, I have a habit of changing subjects without notice. Your names are so similar, especially yours and Keagan's. How did you know when your parents were yelling for you and not him?"

He laughed. "Well, if they were yelling, it was either at me or Killian. The other three were pretty well-behaved. Kerrick and Keagan learned from my mistakes, and our sister, Keara, learned from Killian's. They say shit rolls downhill, but so do lessons. I think Kerrick and Keagan felt every last one of my dad's belt licks as well as I did, even though they weren't on the receiving end."

"So you were a troublemaker?"

"'Were' implies the past, darlin'." He gifted me with a big smile and a wink. "What about you? Out of prison for a day and almost back in. Why?"

"I was trying to avoid you. You obviously don't like me much, so when I saw you there sitting at the bar, I thought I could slip out the back door. That didn't go so well for me."

"That guy got what he deserved. You got him pretty good." The colt followed him like a dog on a leash. I did the same, without the leash.

"I broke his nose." I could still hear the crack of his bones in my head.

"I busted his lip." Keanan lifted his hand to give me a high-five. "You bruised his ego. I think that's the hardest thing for a man to heal."

"Sounds like you have some bruised ego experience. Want to talk about her?"

That simple question rebuilt—and fortified— every wall that had crumbled in the past hour. The warmth in Keanan's eyes turned icy cold, and a frigid leave-me-alone attitude moved over us like an ice storm. I was instantly filled with regret for having pried into his life.

We walked the rest of the way to the ranch in silence. Once there, he turned toward the stables, pulling the colt behind him. He didn't offer me a goodbye, a wave, or even the courtesy of a look.

Chapter 6

I was just getting ready to start season three
of *The Vampire Diaries* when someone knocked at
my door. Figuring it was one of the girls, I didn't
bother to throw on pants. I glided across the tile
floor *Risky Business*-style in a T-shirt, underwear,
and socks. I threw open the door and said,
"What's up, biatch?" Not one of the girls stood
there. Instead, I was looking at the face of
Keanan, and he was looking at most of me.

Karma's the biatch.

"What do you want?"

I hated that I sounded angry, but I was angry. I
thought we'd been making progress. For an hour
or so there in the field, we had connected.
I *knew* we did—and then a glacier covered him

and he froze me out. My life was screwed up enough that I didn't need someone else messing with it, too.

He pulled off his Stetson and held it in one hand by his thigh. I'd never had a thing for cowboys, but this one did something to my insides. I wasn't sure whether it was bad or good. All I knew was he made me feel something, and that was more than I'd felt in years.

"Can I come in?" There were those warm eyes again. The brown specks shimmered under the porch light. "We need to talk."

"I've got nothing to say to you." I stepped back and shut the door, but it caught on the toe of his boot now pushed inside my cabin. "You can't pull me in and push me away. I'm not your toy."

"You don't understand," he said. "I can't just—" He stopped short. "No matter how much I want to." He ran his hand through those sexy black curls. "Ah shit. I've got a lot to say to you, but it can wait."

He pushed the door wide open, stepped inside, and kicked it shut with his boot. He stalked toward me like a feral animal, but I didn't feel in danger. What I felt was heat racing through my body like I was too close to the fire, but I didn't care if I got burned.

I stepped back, and he moved forward, only this time his arms wrapped around me and his mouth covered mine. That kiss sent bolts of awareness to every cell in my body. My nipples tightened, and my core clenched as his tongue demanded entry into my mouth. This was a man who could take what he wanted, but he wouldn't have to. I'd give him anything he asked for.

His tongue pressed past my lips, and I opened for him. He tasted like honey and fear. Like somehow kissing me was breaking every rule in his book. His exploration was thorough, and by the moans coming from his chest, he was enjoying the kiss as much as I was. Well, maybe not, since this was my first kiss in over five years.

Our teeth bumped, and he changed positions. My hair was gripped in his hand so he could steer me where he wanted me. I melted into his touch. He pulled my bottom lip into his mouth and sucked until it stung. Then he went back to kissing me like his life or mine depended on it. Little nibbles followed by the gentle caress of his velvet tongue made my body hum with want and need.

Gently but firmly, he pushed me with his body against the hallway wall. The length of his arousal pressed hard against my hip. One of us groaned, or maybe we both did. He backed away, but I ran my hands down his sides and pulled at his hips, letting him know I wanted him next to me.

We didn't speak. Lord knows that hadn't worked out well for us so far. We used our hands to communicate. I gripped his firm ass through his jeans and pulled him tight to me while I rolled my hips into his.

"Fuck."

"Yes."

It looked like we were down to grunts, and groans, and one-word responses. And then we were on the move. "Your room?"

I turned us around without breaking contact, and I pulled him down the hallway to my bedroom. He walked me back until my knees collapsed against the mattress and his weight covered me.

God, it felt great to be blanketed by a man. His hips against mine. His big, thick thigh pressed between my legs. His mouth moved lower to a spot that made my body shake—that tender patch of skin that sat in the depression of my collarbone. He kissed and nibbled while I practically dry humped his leg.

"More," I panted while I frantically pulled his

shirt from his pants. I wanted my hands all over this man.

"Are you sure?" He leaned up and gave me a look that said, *If we continue, we aren't stopping.* Or at least that was my interpretation of the look because my body was turned to full steam ahead, even though my mind screamed *brakes—brakes.*

"Positive."

I managed to get his shirt off and actually took a second to take him in. Broad-chested and built like a brick wall, he had muscles on top of muscles covered by a dusting of hair that was both soft and prickly at the same time.

I explored each ripple and indentation with my fingertips, brushing the pads over his nipples and watching them pucker while he sucked a hiss through his teeth.

My nipples ached like the soft cotton of my T-shirt had turned to sandpaper and was chafing my skin.

"Fair is fair." I didn't know what that meant until he had the hem of my shirt nearly over my head. "Fuck." His hands cupped me, letting my nipples fall between two fingers. Each time he kneaded my breasts, those fingers squeezed the ache in my stone hard nipples. "You have beautiful breasts, Robyn."

I liked the way some words came from his mouth. One thing was certain. When Keanan McKinley was aroused, his Irish accent flooded forward and words like *breasts* and *beautiful* became dipped in sexy. And my name—oh Lord, just hearing it roll off his tongue brought me close to orgasm.

Then his heat seared me. His tongue rolled around my nipple, and I nearly came undone. He sucked and pulled until it hurt, but I asked for more. He moved to the other and did the same, and I begged him to bite and nip and nibble until he had his fill.

The heat of his tongue ran down my stomach and traced the scar across my ribs. What once caused me so much pain was now the source of my pleasure. Wet and wild, he trailed down to my stomach and dipped his tongue into my belly button. It was an odd sensation that sent a tingle to my clit. Could the two be connected somehow? If so, I'd missed a huge opportunity for self-stimulation.

Finally, he was there, hovering over my core. His face inches from the one place I needed him the most. His thumbs pushed under the less-than-sexy prison-issue cotton panties, and he yanked them over my hips and down my legs where he started a new assault with his tongue at my ankles and moved up.

"Fuck me," I begged.

"I will, darlin'. The first time will be hard and fast. The rest, we'll take them as they come."

His big hands pressed against my thighs, forcing them open so his shoulders could fit between my legs, and then I felt it. The heat of his tongue scorched me as it worked its way through my slit to my clit. Hot and demanding, he lapped at me like a man who had skipped supper.

I had a fleeting thought about my untrimmed bush, but that was gone the minute he pulled my clit inside his mouth and rolled his tongue around it. My hands gripped the sheets, and I hung on for my life. Powerful and potent, this man drew me forward and pushed me back until I begged him to release me.

"Keanan, please." My hips chased his mouth like a moth does a flame.

"You're dripping wet, Robyn." He lifted up, and I could see my juices on his face.

"Finish it."

"Finish?" he said with his heaviest accent yet. "We're nowhere near finished. We're just getting started." He buried his head between my legs again, and this time his relentless sucking and nipping and pulling sent me over the edge.

It was a long way down, and I relished every shudder and twitch and contraction until I couldn't take it anymore. "Stop. No more." I pulled at his hair and tried to press my legs closed, but Keanan was in control, and it appeared I would be finished only when he said so.

I willed my body to relax, and it did for a second before the next wave of heat started to build in my core. It swirled and floated around like a dust bunny caught in a breeze. This wasn't the same as before. This was a slow, steady build, not a race to the finish. He wasn't sucking the pleasure from me but coaxing it one stroke at a time. I didn't tense up and pull it forward; I let it wash over me in wave after wave of pure ecstasy. I knew it had been five years since I'd had an orgasm with someone else, but never in my life had it felt like this.

When he was finished, he rose up and wiped the moisture from his mouth with the back of his hand. "That was beautiful." He toed off his boots and unbuckled his pants. The denim dropped from his waist. He reached for his wallet to get the foil-wrapped package.

I watched as he rolled it on his massive length.

Any other day I might have been scared, but he'd licked the tension and care from my body. He climbed between my legs. "I need it fast and hard." His voice was rough and gravelly, and it vibrated over my body in the most delicious way.

I was like soft putty on the mattress. Fast and hard. Slow and soft. He'd given me so much pleasure already, he could have it any way he wanted it.

"Take me," I gasped. He pressed in, but he didn't get too far. Not only was he long, he was as thick as a salami. "Oh, God."

"You're too damn tight." He pressed forward and pulled back until inch by inch he buried himself inside me.

"So full."

I'd never felt so complete. He filled me to overflowing with his size. He stretched me to the point of pleasure and almost pain, and I loved it; every inch of this man was buried inside me, and I wanted more. I pulled at the rock hard globes of his ass and pulled him until his balls slapped my bottom.

"You ready?"

I was just getting used to the feel of him when he pulled out and slammed back into me. The first time was a shock, like being torn in half from the inside yet somehow not painful, because every stroke after that gave me the feeling of him stitching me together one deep plunge at a time.

He said it would be hard and fast, but it wasn't. Hard—yes. Fast—only his pace. He pressed in again and again until my insides began to quiver.

"You close?"

I bit my lip and nodded. My eyes closed, and I reached for the cliff, hoping we could sail over it together. His hips hit mine, and there was no doubt tomorrow I'd wear the bruises of a night well spent.

"Come with me, darlin'."

His pace picked up, and his power increased until I was there. My pussy clenched tight around him, and I felt it flutter and spasm. He pressed deep and stilled. His face fell slack, and his eyes took on a look of pure bliss, but it was his moans of satisfaction that hit me the hardest. I'd never heard a man sound so satisfied.

He rolled over and fell to his back. I turned to my side and flopped my arm across his chest. Everything in my body ached so good.

"I'll be right back."

He rolled out of bed and walked to the bathroom. I let out a laugh when I realized we were both still wearing socks.

"You won't be laughing tomorrow."

He climbed back in bed and spooned up behind me. I knew he was right. Tomorrow, I'd be lucky if I could walk.

Chapter 7

My body screamed when I woke up. Keanan might have spooned with me for a few minutes, but it had taken two more hours and three more rounds to wear him out enough to fall asleep.

I rolled over in search of his warm body and came up empty. The bed wasn't only vacant, it was cold, just like the feeling that was seeping into my heart. He'd taken what he wanted and left.

I couldn't be too upset; it wasn't like he hadn't given. In fact, he gave and gave until I couldn't take any more. So why did I feel so hollow and gutted?

I padded into the kitchen and set the cup up to brew, put in a pod, and pressed the button.

While it hissed and spit out oil-black liquid, I walked to the bathroom in desperate need of a hot shower.

The water cascaded over me. The heat relaxed sore muscles; the water pressure released tension. I analyzed every possible reason he could have for sneaking out of my bed.

He had work to do.

He couldn't sleep.

He didn't want the awkward morning after.

He regretted being with me.

There was no doubt the sex was great for both of us, but in the end, Keanan was holding back. He came to my door last night saying he couldn't, even if he wanted to, and yet he did—four times.

I couldn't work this out on my own. I needed Mickey and her oatmeal to put the pieces together.

Once I was dressed, I doctored up my coffee and stepped outside into a beautiful sunny day. The sounds of horses and the smell of fresh cut grass filled the air. It didn't feel like home yet, but it felt familiar, and that was comforting.

A hunk of a man who was leading a horse to the stables stopped at the sight of me. "You must be Robyn." He transferred the reins of the horse into his left hand and wiped his palm on his jeans before he shook my hand. "I'm Cole." That was mighty sweet of him and darn considerate considering I had just showered.

I tucked my hair behind my ear. "Nice to meet you, Cole." I glanced around the property. There seemed to be more people here than yesterday. "It's getting crazy around here."

"Just wait until the rest of the guests show up."

"You sound as excited as I feel." I pasted on a smile, and he laughed. "Lots of guests means lots of work, but if I know Mickey, it also means lots of alcohol, music, food, and fun."

"Sounds like a good trade-off."

I glanced toward the main house, where I knew some steel-cut oats were sitting in a crockpot waiting for me. "Nice to meet you."

"You, too, Robyn. Don't be a stranger." He gave me that I'd-like-to-get-to-know-you-better look, but I'd been warned about him from the girls. He was the Casanova who never stopped trying.

I walked past a white tent that was going up in front of the arena. Mickey had mentioned something about outdoor seating. I still couldn't believe she was getting married.

I entered the house and looked around. The

table was full but for one seat next to Keanan. Of course.

"Glad you're here," Kerrick said. He rose from his chair and followed me to the crockpot. "I called in the details of yesterday's event. The officer I talked to was a hard ass and has requested you see a specific parole officer. I'm not familiar with this person, but I'm sure they are fair. The courts feel like if you've already had a run-in and you've been out less than a few days, your risk of recidivism is high."

"Jesus Christ." I shoved the spoon into the pot and grabbed a bowl from the counter. "The asshole attacked me." Kerrick lifted his brows like he was questioning the truth of that statement. "You know that's what happened." I looked toward Keanan, who sat with his back turned toward us. "He saw it go down."

I plopped a clump of overcooked oatmeal into the bowl and spooned on some raisins and brown sugar. I knew what I was facing. It was the same thing in court five years ago. Just like I did then, I now stood in front of Kerrick without a scratch on me. So much for learning to protect myself. The simple act of self-defense always seemed to bite me in the ass.

"The officer gave them your phone number,

so you should be hearing from someone soon. I got the impression they want an emergency meeting with you."

Super. I wanted to get out of prison and lie low, but instead, with my recent scuffle in the alleyway, I'd moved to the top of the parole officer's list.

"Thanks, Kerrick. I appreciate your help."

Kerrick leaned on the counter. "I know you were defending yourself. I hate to tell you this, but if you ever find yourself in that situation again, either run like hell or make sure you can prove without a doubt he attacked you. You fight too clean, Robyn." He patted me on the back like a big brother would.

"You're telling me to take a hit."

He let out an exasperated breath and nodded. "The system sucks. By the way, you saved my girl's life. Without your training, she never would have made it out of Morgan's clutches. Without Mickey, a lot of lives would be different." He looked at the table where his brothers sat and chatted while Mickey buried her head in a newspaper. "I can never thank you enough for that."

"You're welcome. I love that woman."

"I do, too. That's why I'm marrying her."

He walked back to the table where there were

a few other men I didn't recognize, plus the one man I couldn't get off my mind. Keanan sat there as if I didn't exist, though I sure as hell existed last night when he was balls deep inside me.

"Good morning," I said as I sat in the chair next to Keanan.

"Mornin'." A young buck stood and offered me his hand. "I'm Toby. Outside of you, I'm the newest addition to the ranch." He pointed to the tall, lanky man sitting across from him. "That there is Tyson, and you know the rest." He glanced over at Keanan. "Have you met Keanan?"

I looked at the man who had become very well-acquainted with me last night. "Oh, yes, Keanan and I..." What was I supposed to say, *We fucked like rabbits all night, but I don't really know him, only his nine-inch cock and his incredibly talented tongue?* No, that would never do, so I finished with, "We have met."

I reached across the table for the pitcher of milk. My breast skimmed Keanan's arm. His eyes shot straight to the spot as if I'd burned him.

"How are you?" I tried to push the hurt out of my voice, but it was there anyway.

"Good. Busy." He gathered his dishes and rose from his seat.

"You're going to leave again?" I hoped my words weren't loud enough for everyone to hear.

"I've got important stuff to do." His chair ground against the wooden floor when he pushed it back.

I'd been hurt by words before, but these ones sliced through my chest like a samurai's sword. He couldn't have wounded me more if he tried. Didn't he know when a woman shared her body, she shared so much more?

"Asshole," I blurted out.

Mickey dropped her paper. "What?"

I shook my head. "I was just hoping my parole officer isn't an asshole."

"Me, too, sister. You'll need a ride. Today, you can take mine." She pulled the keys to her truck from her pocket and tossed them to me. "There's always a set of wheels around. Isn't that right?"

Mickey glared at the guys at the table. I knew very little about cowboys, but I was sure they protected their rides like they protected their horses. No one wanted to hand me their keys, but every single one of them would—except Keanan. He picked his keys up from the table on his way out and shoved them into his pocket.

I couldn't believe I'd let that cold, heartless man into my body. Maybe that was his plan. He needed a warm body to thaw his iciness, and mine had been ready and willing. Live and learn, they said; I did both last night. I lived a little, and I doubled my lifetime total of orgasms. Even Joe could never pull that kind of passion from me. I'd also learned a big lesson, and that was men hadn't evolved in the five years I'd been in prison. If anything, they'd reverted back to their chest-pounding, club-swinging tendencies.

I didn't have time for his shit. I'd have to cut my losses and call myself a victor, regardless. I'd miss his tongue on my clit, but I didn't want to hear another damn word come out of his mouth.

I was at the sink cleaning up the breakfast dishes when my phone rang. "Hello," I answered with some trepidation.

It turned out to be my new probation officer, who happened to be a woman—and she was excited to meet me. Lucky me.

Chapter 8

I drove Mickey's beat up tin can of a truck to the address Lucy had given me. It wasn't the usual type of place I would think an ex-con would meet a parole officer. It was an hour outside of town on a ranch, much like Mickey's.

When I reached the end of the long gravel road, there was a middle-aged woman dealing with some horses. I ground the truck into first gear and killed the engine.

My sneaker covered feet hit the gravel, and I began my walk of doom. Breaking a man's nose wasn't how I wanted to enter my new life, but he'd asked for it—and now I had to pay for it.

"You Robyn?" She patted a horse on the

hindquarters and sent it running in the other direction. Kind of like I wanted to do right now.

"Yes, ma'am. That's me." I offered her my
hand, and she gave me a good shake. Her hands
were weathered and worn and calloused. They
were hardworking hands.

"I'm Lucy, your PO, and you came just in time
to be useful." She walked to a wall where a bunch
of yard tools hung. She tossed me a pitchfork and
told me to follow her.

In the first stall, she directed me to shovel shit
while she came behind me with new hay.

"Let me tell you a few things about myself,"
she said. "I've always been a girl who rode."

She leaned against the wall and watched me
pitch shit and hay into a wheelbarrow. It wasn't
what I had imagined my day would be like, but
this woman had the power to send me back to
Cell Block C, and if shoveling shit would keep me
out, I'd do it.

"Horses?"

"Nope, I was the first woman patched in as a
War Bird. We were a badass group of bikers from
Fury, Colorado. That was until the whole group
got shot up." She pulled the neck of her shirt
down and showed me a chest riddled with bullet

holes. "I was a tough girl who liked to ride free, fuck hard, and push the rules."

"What's that have to do with me?" Lord, this was going to be a long meeting if I had to listen to this woman's life story.

"Nothing. Just thought I'd share. I hear that's a nice thing to do." She let the neck of her shirt go, and it popped back into place. "Anyway, that was over twenty years ago, and that one day changed my life. A loud pop sounded out during a meeting, and everyone reacted rather than acted. Bullets flew like a swarm of buzzards until no one was standing. If you weren't dead, you went to jail because your bullet was found in someone else's body. My bullets were found in two bodies, both members of a rival gang called the Rebels. I got ten years in the state penitentiary, which was a light sentence for two murders. Those bodies were so riddled with bullets, no one could be certain mine were the killing shots."

I had finished shoveling this stall out when she pointed to the next. I lifted the wheelbarrow handles and moved on while she laid out fresh hay. "Your point is?"

"No point. Just sharing some more." She swung her long braid over her shoulder and joined me in the next stall. "There's a lot of shit to pick up in life. You keep shoveling it and shoveling it, and yet it never ends."

Now I was getting her point. "Yep, life is shit. Is that what you're telling me?"

"Nope, just sharing. Anyway, ten years is a long time to spend by yourself. It's a long time to shovel the shit of your own life. Tell me about your shit, Robyn, and why that shit is already piling up high."

I jammed the fork into the sodden hay and lifted it to the wheelbarrow. "I'm a shit magnet. Especially when it comes to men."

I thought about Keanan and stabbed the hay again. Maybe working my frustrations out in the barn would be a better way to deal with them. Lord knew there had to be a lot of shit at Mickey's. And the horses weren't the worst offenders —a certain man there was the biggest shit of them all.

"This isn't about men. It's about you and your experience with them. Tell me something I don't know."

"I beat the shit out a robber and spent five years paying for it."

"I know that. Move on. Tell me why you didn't stop beating him when he was down."

"Probably for the same reason you didn't stop

shooting. We're similar in nature. It's all about self-preservation."

"Nope, that's where you're wrong. I'm a badass. You're a victim. If you were just trying to stop him from entering the studio, you did that when you broke three of his ribs and dislocated his shoulder. You didn't stop there. Something in you snapped, and you didn't stop until you knew he was stopped for good. Whose sins did he pay for?"

I tossed the pitchfork across the stall. "What are you, my fucking shrink?"

"Nope, I'm not qualified for that job. But I am your parole officer, and it appears someone else is going to pay a high price if we don't figure out a plan to unhinge your anger in a productive way." She tossed the pitchfork back at me. "That shit isn't going anywhere until we sift through it."

I worked my way through two more stalls before I spoke again. "Did you know I went to college and studied environmental sciences?"

"No, tell me more. Did you get your degree? Your sheet didn't say you had a degree. Well, not that kind anyway. Just a third-degree black belt."

I mucked my way to the last stall. "I was starting my sophomore year, and it was a late night at the library. I was walking alone between the engineering building and the library when I was attacked." I closed my eyes and let the scene soak in. "I don't know if it was one person or more than one person, but I was too weak to fight him off. He beat me up and stabbed me for twenty dollars and some change."

"Asshole."

I opened my eyes and laughed. "Yes, the fucker didn't even rape me."

She lifted her brow questioningly. "You're unhappy about that?"

"No, but I don't understand it. Who beats a girl to within an inch of her life over twenty freaking dollars?"

"Who found you?"

I smiled at the thought of Joe. "My resident assistant found me. He said he was leaving the library and heard someone scream. He never left me again after that, and I was grateful for his presence. He wasn't happy when I quit school and started martial arts, but I promised myself I'd never be a victim again."

"And yet you are each time a man approaches you."

Not every man, I thought. But then again, Keanan might as well have hit me over the head and taken what he wanted. The pain felt similar.

Lucy grabbed the pitchfork and hung it on the wall. "Let's get cleaned up. I want you to go somewhere with me."

We went into her house and washed up. She came out of a room with two pairs of boots. "You can't go in sneakers. At least fake it till you make it." She tossed me both pairs. "One's a seven, one's an eight." I slid on the eights and pulled my jeans over the brown, tooled leather. "Those look good on you. You can keep them. Saves me the hassle of sending them back."

We climbed into her truck, a big black beast that looked new and had a decent radio and air conditioning.

"Thank for the boots."

"No worries. I figured you already earned them. Now tell me about yesterday."

"I was protecting myself." I leaned into the door and watched the world whiz by at sixty-five miles an hour.

"Okay, was that yourself of today or yourself of twenty years ago?"

"Is there a difference?"

"Yes, a big one." She took a right onto a two-lane country road.

"The guy pulled a knife on me."

"I hear you broke his nose and somebody else busted his lip, maybe a few teeth."

"Are you saying I'm wrong to fight back?"

"Nope, all I'm saying is make sure you know which girl you are when you're fighting. Who were you yesterday?"

I looked out at the open prairie. Miles of open plains in front of me, and everything was all clear. "I was me, the Robyn today who wasn't going to be the same victim I was twenty years ago. I warned him. I tried to talk him out of what he was doing. He attacked, and I acted."

"Perfect. I've got no problem with you acting on a threat. I've got a huge issue with you reacting. There's a difference."

I pondered her statement. "You're right."

"I know." She pulled her truck into a lot full of similar vehicles and hopped out. "Let's go look at some horseflesh." She rounded the front of the truck. "The man flesh isn't bad to look at either."

"Why are we here?"

"Because I have other interests than making sure ex-cons like you stay out of jail. I run a ranch, and ranches can't be called ranches without animals. My animals of choice are horses. Just like the ranch you're living at. You've got a sweet deal there. Don't fuck it up."

She charged off to where a group of cowboys stood at a fence while horse after horse was paraded through the ring.

"I never thought I'd say it, but I like this. There's an energy to the ranch you don't feel anywhere else. These people care about what they're doing; they care about the animals. It's like a part of them."

"I'm not surprised you feel it," Lucy said. "These are the best people in the world, especially that man. He's got something really special going on in Wyoming. Best damn ranch in the Rockies. Puts us all to shame." She pointed to a man standing by himself in the corner.

That man, of course, was Keanan.

My whole body shuddered at the sight of him. I wanted to stomp up to him and shove the toe of my new size-eight boot up his ass, but I also wanted to pull him to me and let him kiss the air from my lungs. I hated being conflicted.

Instead of giving him any more energy, though, I turned my attention to Lucy and listened to her talk about the horses and why one was better than the other. She explained how they're measured by hands, which made no sense to me.

Once the horses were gone, she clapped her hands and said, "Now for the fun."

I followed her into an arena where the bidding started. She held up her paddle and lowered it enough times to give her arthritis. When she won the bid, she squealed like a little kid. There was so much excitement, I almost forgot about the smoking hot man who was just steps away from me. Almost. When I turned to look at him, he was right beside me.

"Robyn. We need to talk."

"We really don't," I answered. I turned to Lucy and told her I'd meet her outside, then moved to leave. Keanan followed me.

I walked to Lucy's truck, hoping he'd turn off in another direction and leave me alone, but he didn't.

"Don't act like a baby. Talk to me."

"You want to talk now?" I shoved my hands in my jean pockets. It was safer for him that way. "Why now?"

"Because we need to talk." He approached me, and out of instinct I took a fighter's stance. His eyes went wide, and he stepped back. When I remembered Lucy's talk, though, I stood down and shoved my hands back into my pockets.

"No. We. Don't." The words came out like a growl. "You wouldn't talk to me this morning."

"I want to talk to you now." He held out his hands in the same way a person does to a strange dog. Like I was supposed to smell him and know he was safe, but I knew he wasn't. He could break more than my body—he could break my heart.

"We aren't about talking, Keanan. We're about fucking. That's all I am to you. A quick, secret fuck."

"Sweetheart, there was nothing quick about us." He bit his bottom lip in that all-too-sexy way, and I wanted to rip it from his teeth and bite it harder. But I knew if his lip ended up in my mouth, the next step was his cock in my body.

"You got what you wanted. It was fun. Move on."

"It's not like that," he said. "If you only knew the truth, the reasons I can't –"

"Then tell me."

"I can't do that either." He gave me a look of regret, then turned and walked away.

Chapter 9

"Let's meet next week. You can explain to me why Keanan McKinley looked like he laid his heart out to you and you stomped on it in your new boots." Lucy had driven me back to her ranch, and I was getting ready to head back to Mickey's.

"It's not like that. He started something, I finished it."

Lucy shook her head. "That man didn't look like whatever you two had going on was finished."

I gave Lucy a hug and changed the subject. "Thanks for everything. Am I squared away about yesterday?"

"Yep, just make sure this Robyn stays in

charge. She's older and wiser, and she'll make better decisions."

I climbed into Mickey's truck and turned over the engine. "I will."

"And Robyn, cut Keanan some slack. I hear he's a good man."

I waved out the window as I drove away and thought to myself, *It depends on what your scale's measuring. In bed, he's an eleven. Otherwise, I'd give him a three.*

I was halfway back to Mickey's when the tire blew out. I pulled the truck over to the side of the road to check for further damage.

I'd never changed a tire before, so I had no idea what that would entail, but I knew it was useless when I unwrapped the spare and found it flat, too. And as luck would have it, I was stranded on the one stretch of highway without cell coverage.

Better get walking.

I made it about a half-mile when I heard the gravel crunch behind me. I swiveled around to see who was approaching, and I snarled. Of course it was Keanan. Who else would it be?

He pulled up next to me. "I saw Mickey's truck. I can help with the flat."

"I don't need your help." I continued to walk. He continued to drive beside me.

"It's six miles back to the ranch. Even somebody as stubborn as you can't walk that," he said.

"Watch me," I answered.

Bad choice of words—he got back in that damn truck and crept alongside me. And then came confirmation that the universe did indeed hate me: it started raining. The rain didn't come down in sprinkles; it came down in a torrent, and I had no choice but to get in his truck or drown. So, I climbed inside the clean, warm truck that smelled of Keanan and tried my best to ignore him.

I leaned against the door and watched the water stream down the window. It was silent, and it stayed that way until Keanan purposely passed the entrance to the ranch.

"What are you doing?"

"Going for a ride," he answered.

"Against my will." I turned toward him and crossed my arms over my chest. "Which is called kidnapping."

"Call the police, then." He drove through the field where we had come across the troublesome colt. "My brother called and told me that damn colt was missing. I figured I could find him, and I needed your help to get him back."

"Why me?"

"He seems to like you." He pulled into the center of the field, whose formerly dry grass was sagging with the weight of the now-passed storm's water. "I guess it's because you're kind of the same. Neither of you really knows where you belong. You both just know it's not here."

I had nothing to say to that, or at least nothing he deserved to hear. So, in silence we both got out to look for the colt. After twenty minutes, we found him limping near the fence. It turned out he'd made himself lame from all his escapes.

Keanan leaned down and picked up the colt, draping him over his shoulders. A set of legs hung on each side of his head. I walked beside them and talked to the poor thing, trying to calm him down.

Together, we put him in the back of Keanan's truck, and he asked me to sit with the poor beast during the ride back to the stables. I was happy to do so. I much preferred Houdini's company to Keanan's. The little guy seemed to like me just as much. The only way to keep him calm during the ten-minute drive to Second Chance Ranch was to let Houdini rest his head on my lap.

Before we left, Keanan had called his brother and asked for the vet to meet us at the ranch. When we arrived, sure enough, a tall blond man approached and helped Keanan pull the horse from the bed of the truck.

When he smiled at me and said, "I'm Roland, Natalie's man," my gut clenched at how proud he sounded to declare himself hers, while this man behind me wouldn't even talk to me in front of others.

"I'm Robyn." I followed them into the barn, where Roland had a corner dedicated to his work.

"Nice to meet you. I've heard amazing stuff about you."

I wanted to hear the prognosis, so I stood off to the side and watched the men work. First they dried the colt off, then Keanan held him down while Roland cleaned the open wound, applied salve, and bandaged the injury.

Once that was done, Roland turned to me and said, "He needs to be enclosed so he can't get loose. If he doesn't get an infection, he should heal up fine."

Once I knew the little guy had a fighting chance, I was okay with leaving. "You seem to have it all under control. I'm going home."

"Stay," Keanan demanded.

He lifted the colt from the table and placed him in a stall whereby all accounts he wouldn't be able to escape, but then again, he'd earned the name Houdini because of his disappearing skills.

Roland grabbed his stuff and headed out the door, calling, "You know where to find me if something changes with the colt."

Once Roland was out of sight, Keanan grabbed me and kissed me hard. Before I could react, he pulled me into a room off to the side of the barn. Inside were wooden horses and blankets. He tossed one on the ground and laid me back. I knew I should get up and leave, but my body said no. It wanted what it wanted, and it wanted Keanan.

"You are so damn beautiful."

His words sang in my ears and my heart. How long had it been since a man declared me beautiful?

"I need you now, lass." And there was that Irish accent again to make fire race through my veins. He pulled and yanked at my jeans until they caught at my ankles and wouldn't go past my boots. "Fuck it," he cursed.

"Yes," I whispered. In seconds, he was wrapped and ready.

"I want you, Robyn, in more ways than you can imagine." His voice was strong and fierce and possessive.

My knees fell open. It was my way of submitting to his request without a word, and then he was inside me. Deep inside me, but this wasn't the urgent fucking we'd done last night. This was different. Sure he was powerful and large, and each thrust moved me inches on the blanket, but it was like he was determined to make sure I knew he was there. Determined to make sure I never forgot how it felt to have him between my legs. Determined to remind me what it felt like to be his, if only for that moment. I knew right then I'd never have a lover like Keanan McKinley again.

"God, Robyn. You're so fucking right. And you're so fucking wrong, and my head is so screwed up, I don't know if I'm coming or going." He drove into me again and again until my body began to shudder.

"You're coming," I told him breathlessly, then yelled, "I'm coming!" as I sailed off the edge with this man again. My whole body quaked, but he didn't let up. He pounded into me again and again until minutes later I was back at the edge and shaking like a crack whore in need of a fix.

KELLY COLLINS

"You like my cock in you?" He leaned down and kissed me, taking in my bottom lip and sucking it until it burned. Then he let it loose.

"Yes. I love it in me." I gripped his muscled arms and hung on while he reminded me of what it was like to have sex with him. Long. Hard. Thick. Fierce.

"Mine, and no one else's." That sounded more like a demand than a question.

I reached up and whispered against his lips. "Only yours." And then I bit his lower lip for making me feel so shitty early. He groaned and kissed me again. This time, his tongue probed my mouth for minutes until I was a hot mess of unspent energy below him.

"You want to come again for me?"

My head rolled from side to side as he drove into me over and over again. "Yes!"

I cried. My body buzzed with tension. It was like a frayed electrical wire, zinging and zapping at anything that touched it. A slight wind would have sent me over the edge, but it was his words that sent me soaring.

"I could fall in love with you if I let myself." He pressed his thumb against my clit, and we both soared together, and when it was over, he didn't disappear this time. He helped me up and walked with me hand in hand to my cabin. Just before we entered, he said, "We need to talk. There's something I need to tell you." And my heart tumbled from my chest to my new boots.

Chapter 10

I walked to the refrigerator like I was walking to my hanging. There was something so startling in his statement that my hands shook as I grabbed two beers from the middle shelf.

Earlier, I'd been mad at him for not talking to me, and now I wasn't sure whether I wanted to hear anything he had to say. But I owed him an ear, and when he was finished, I'd decide whether I owed him a kick in the ass, too, because if he told me another *he just couldn't*, I was going to turn into a third girl no one had seen. The Robyn who wasn't going to put up with Keanan's shit. That Robyn would send him packing with a brand-new, size-eight pair of women's Ariat boots so far up his ass, he'd need medical help to remove them.

I walked into the living room to find him sitting on the sofa. He patted the cushion beside him, but I took the seat across from him. It was more for his protection than my comfort. I popped the top on my beer and took a long drink.

"You wanted to tell me something?"

"I *need* to tell you something."

My stomach twisted and turned into knots. I leaned back and kicked those boots up on the table just so he could see how big a size eight really was.

"I was in love once." He popped open his beer and sucked back some suds. "I'd known her since we were little kids. She was the girl next door, and I thought I'd marry her and grow old with her and all that bullshit."

"Okay, so you think love is bullshit." I rocked the pointed toe of my boot back and forth. It was itching to make contact.

"After high school, we went to college. She changed there and got hooked on drugs and ended up turning to petty theft to support the habit. She wound up in and out of jail several times."

"So it's not me you hate. It's the fact that I was

in jail." That came as both a relief and a worry. I couldn't change the past; all I could do was build a future.

"I don't hate you. I like you too much. I just don't trust you or your type."

"My type?" My voice rose an octave. "Tell me what type that is."

"The type that will probably end up back in a cell." He leaned forward and crushed his empty beer can on the table. "Liz couldn't be saved. I tried, but in the end she did anything to get her fix. She cheated on me, she stole from me, and in the end she left me for a fifteen-year sentence. I can't do that again."

"And you think I'm her?"

"No, I'm asking you to tell me who you are. I'm asking you to tell me you'll never be her."

Oh, I was angry. I was angry with myself for falling for this man, and I was angry with some faceless woman for fucking him up. I was angry at the asshole who started this twenty years ago when he attacked me. I was just plain damn angry.

"Here's the problem, Keanan: I like you. I could like you more if you weren't such an ass-hole, but I'm not her. I'm not a drug addict— never used a drug in my life, and I never will. I'm just a girl who was beaten to within an inch of her life and left to die over twenty bucks. The only men I've been with since that day were the guy who saved me and you. I'm not asking you to save me. Only I can do that for myself. I'm asking you to trust me. If you can't, there's the door. Don't let it hit you in the ass on the way out."

He rushed in front of me and laid his head in my lap. This big, burly man was in a position of submission, and it broke my heart for him. I knew what it was like to love and lose. I'd watched my ex-fiancé drive away a few days ago. I was no longer in love with him—that had ended when I got the letter that said he'd married—but I loved what we'd been together, and that was a solid couple against a cruel world. I twisted my fingers through Keanan's curls and knew I could have that again with him. If he'd let me.

That night, he made love to me slowly, and when I woke the next morning, he was there wrapped around my body. For the first time in years, I felt like I was home. It wasn't a place. Home, for me, was a person, and that was Keanan.

LATER THAT DAY, I was back in the bridal shop for Mickey's final fitting. The fabulous five were together in one place again, and it felt wonderful.

Holly sat on the bench and rubbed her stomach while I watched it roll under her fingertips.

"What does that feel like inside?" I took a seat beside her, and she pulled my hand to her belly.

"Like a hamster running in a wheel after he ate a bag of Cheetos and drank a bottle of pop."

Something hard moved under my fingertips, and I laughed. "Alien is more like it."

She smiled like she'd won the lottery. They all had. I'd never seen these four women look so complete.

Megan grabbed a gaudy gown from the rack and twirled it around her body. "What do you think?" she asked with no hint of seriousness.

Natalie fanned her face, and in her best Scarlett O'Hara voice she said, "Why, Megan, I don't know nothin' about birthin' no babies, but I do know this dress won't work anywhere but on a plantation like Tara." She swooned and fell onto the bench next to Holly.

The saleswoman brought Mickey's dress from the back and put it in a room for her to try on. I hadn't seen it yet and couldn't wait.

While she changed, she talked behind the door. "Do you guys remember Coolie Craig?"

Megan started laughing. She'd always been the quiet one, but living with Killian had brought her out of her shell. "Yes, she talked about her nine-inch man. We all thought he was real until she showed us a picture of a G.I. Joe action figure."

We laughed together.

"What about Ida? She's the one who made almost real looking dicks out of Kotex and latex gloves." We all turned to look at Natalie. "What? So, I tested the product. Desperate times and all that. Of course, the real deal is always better." She blushed slightly, which was odd because I didn't think Natalie could blush.

"She's the one you should have given the cucumber to," I said to Mickey, who was still dressing behind the door.

"You gave her a cucumber?" Holly asked. "She put a jumbo dick in my drawer."

Natalie and Megan laughed.

"They put one in my drawer, too, with a lifetime supply of D batteries."

"So, it's been useful?" Mickey asked from inside the dressing room.

I considered not saying anything about me and Keanan, but these were my sisters, and we shared everything. "There's no point in using a toy when you can have the real thing."

All eyes snapped to me. Even Mickey peeked her head out the door. "Who?"

Names were bouncing around the room from everyone.

"Cole?"

"Tyson?"

"Toby?"

I continued to shake my head.

Mickey stepped out of the dressing room looking like a gossamer princess. The dress was perfect, and the white blinged-out boots were amazing. You can take the girl from the ranch, but you'd never take the ranch from Mickey.

All talk of my mystery man ceased to exist for a moment. Everyone was up, walking around Mickey in awe.

"You sure do clean up nice for a criminal," I said.

Those were the exact words Keanan said to me when he saw me in this same room days ago. I wondered whether he'd felt like I did right then. Like I was looking at something so beautiful, it hurt my chest. Mickey was stunning.

She pressed her hands down the front of the dress. "Is it okay?"

We all nodded in silence because there were
no words to describe her. How could you describe perfection?

"Well, now that this is done," Mickey says, "we
can talk about Robyn fucking Keanan."

No one looked at Mickey anymore. All eyes
were on me, and I wanted to crawl up under
Mickey's dress and hide.

As soon as the heat in my cheeks subsided, I
raised my eyes toward the group of women I'd
grown to love.

While Megan helped Mickey out of the dress,
the rest gave me that look that said, *Spill the beans.*

"It's nothing, really. We don't even like each
other." That was kind of the truth. The only good
thing about the two of us was the sex.

All four women piped in at the same time, but
their response was the same: that none of them
had initially gotten along with the men they were
with now.

"Yeah, but which of you wanted to murder
him one second and make love to him the next?" I
asked.

They all raised their hands. I was so screwed.

Mickey came out of the dressing room in
jeans and her everyday boots. "They get you with
the sex. Feed a starving animal, and they're a fan

for life." She pointed to my boots and tilted her head in question.

"Gift from my PO after she made me muck out ten stalls."

"You want to rope him for life? Wear those and nothing else," Mickey said.

The girls nodded like a row of bobblehead dolls, then Natalie chimed in. "But if you fall in love with Keanan, you'll leave us."

I watched the light dim from all the girls' eyes. Surely, they had to know. "I was never going to stay. This is a stopping point. But no matter where I land, I'll always be in touch. Besides, I'm not really Keanan's type."

Mickey rolled her eyes. "You have a vagina; he's a McKinley. You're his type. Also, those men can't resist the fabulous five. Why?"

We all came together in a huddle like they did in sports and stuck a hand in the middle. On three, we shouted, "Because we're fabulous!"

WHEN WE GOT BACK to the ranch, I headed straight for my cabin. Mickey had said something that resonated—to wear the boots and nothing else—but that had also made me think about how lazy I'd been with myself. Since the day I arrived, I'd worn nothing but jeans and sported a ponytail. Keanan hadn't seen the me I could be.

I rushed to my room and the closet the girls had filled for me with clothes I'd ignored because I dressed for my mood, which had been bad at best.

Instead of the closet, I was drawn to a note on my bed. A bed I'd left unmade this morning and now was put together like a housekeeper from a fine hotel had been here.

Robyn,

I came back for a kiss and found you missing. I'm told you were out with the girls. I was hoping I could persuade you to take a chance and come out with me. Dinner tonight at seven?

Keanan

After his name was his cell number. I stared at it for a moment. A kaleidoscope of butterflies fluttered in my stomach. Was this the same man who'd ignored me yesterday? Maybe Keanan was starting to see beyond my past to the woman I had always been and could be for him.

Just as I was typing in the word *yes* to the number he left, my phone rang. It was a blocked number, but I answered anyway.

"Hello?"

The only thing I heard was someone's heavy, raspy breath. I looked down at the phone as if it would reveal something, but it didn't. I listened again, and a chill ran up my spine and caused the tiny hairs of my neck to stand straight up.

I pressed end and flopped on my bed. Who the hell would do that? My first thoughts went to Keanan, but I dismissed that. He wasn't a heavy-breather type. Then I thought of the man I'd paralyzed and Tipsy Ted, and a feeling of doom spread across my limbs.

Chapter 11

At exactly seven, there was a knock at the door. I looked at myself in the mirror one more time. It had been years since I'd worn a dress. I never felt comfortable in them after the attack. But tonight was special. Tonight was my first date since high school. Sure, I'd been out with Joe dozens of times, but that kind of evolved. After the accident, he was just there all the time. He never left. It wasn't something we talked about, it was assumed.

He never even asked me to marry him; he just told me I would be his wife, and I agreed. There was no engagement, no ring—just a nod and an expectation.

This was different. Keanan asked me on a

date, and even though I had no intention of saying "no," I had the option. It was funny how until now, I'd never thought about how limited my life was with Joe. I had thought he made it full, but now I saw the difference.

He knocked again, and in hopes of calming my heartbeat, I pressed my hands against the sweetheart neckline of the little red sundress —*little* being the operative word since its length was only mid-thigh. As a girl who wore mostly jeans and long-sleeved shirts, I felt damn near naked.

I took a big breath and flung open the door. Standing in front of me was a real, live cowboy, from his polished boots all the way to the white pearly snaps of his freshly pressed Western shirt. And those black jeans made my insides churn with heat. They gripped his thighs like a hungry lover.

"You look beautiful, Robyn." He reached out and twirled the curl in my hair around his fingers. I'd gone all out, from curling my hair to trimming my pubes. Even my toenails were painted with a pink color called *Suck Me There*. Natalie had brought it by after she heard about my date.

"You ready, darlin'?" He offered me his arm. I

picked up my purse, and we walked out connected at the hip. He helped me into the truck where a single red rose sat on my seat. I picked it up and smelled it. It was sweet and fragrant.

"It's beautiful."

"Hardly compares to you."

He left me with that thought and walked around the truck. I couldn't keep my eyes off him. If this hadn't been an important step in our budding relationship, I would've just dragged him back inside and into my bed.

He climbed into the driver's side smelling like sin and spice.

"I'm told the only date-worthy place to dine is Trevi's. Is a steakhouse all right with you?" He started the truck, and the diesel engine rumbled to life. As we pulled out, several heads popped out of their doors, including Mickey and Kerrick.

"You told them you were taking me on a date?"

He reached over, grabbed my hand, and threaded his fingers through mine. "I'm proud to take you on a date."

"What changed? Just yesterday, you were embarrassed to be seen with me."

He squeezed my fingers gently. "I was never embarrassed about you. I was just unsure I wanted to pursue someone with your past. You know the saying. Once bitten, twice shy."

"I never bite."

"Never say never, darlin'. I like a good nibble on occasion."

"I'll remember that."

"Please do."

We arrived at Trevi's, where Keanan asked me to wait until he opened my door. He was pulling out all the stops. He picked me up from the high truck and kissed me before he let me slide down his body. Then he proudly walked me into the restaurant like I was a prize filly. I now know why the girls fell so hard and fast for their men. They were like a triple-chocolate brownie dipped in hot fudge and sprinkles. Like a good brownie, they did have the crusty outside, but also the delicious soft interior.

We were seated in a quiet corner table lit by candlelight. He pulled out my chair, and when he pushed it in, he bent over and kissed my neck. Oh, he already knew the spot that drove me wild —that little crater of soft skin that sat by my collarbone. There was a braid of nerves that connected that spot directly to my sex, and the minute his lips touched, every cell tingled.

He took his seat across from me. He was too

far away, but I was glad because the distance meant I wouldn't end up back in the slammer for indecent exposure. Those few feet kept me from stripping off my clothes and riding his cock until I screamed.

Keanan ordered a bottle of wine while I looked over the menu.

"I hear they have good meat." Keanan said this straight-faced, but I laughed.

"I know where to find good meat." I lifted my brows and stared at the table as if it weren't there, my eyes glued to where I knew his package was.

"So we could have stayed home, and you'd have been happy?"

God, yes. But that wasn't the point of this dinner. Keanan was making a statement. A big one. And I appreciated the overture.

I sipped the wine the waiter had just delivered and looked over my glass into his eyes. They were often steely gray, but tonight they shimmered baby blue, and I wondered whether they changed with his mood. Tonight, he seemed lighter and brighter, just like his eyes.

"No, I understand what it took for you to ask me on this date. I don't see you as a risk taker, and I'm a risk. I appreciate everything this date means."

He lifted his glass and nodded. "I'd still like to show you my meat later." His eyes sparkled while he tried to hold back his smile.

The waiter approached to take our order, and I thought I'd give Keanan a hard time.

"I'm a bit of a carnivore," I said. I toed off my boot while I spoke and raised my *Suck Me There*-painted toes to sit between Keanan's legs. "Can you tell me which piece of meat is the biggest? I really like a juicy, high-end cut in my mouth."

Keanan moved in his seat to adjust his hardening length. One of his hands moved beneath the table to hold my foot still.

"There's the T-bone and the porterhouse."

"Oh, yes," I cooed. "I really like the bone." I freed my foot from his grasp and ran it down the length of his shaft.

"She'll have the T-bone, and I'll have the porterhouse," he said in a pained voice. "If she doesn't like hers, I'll feed her my meat." He snapped the menus closed and shoved them toward the waiter.

"You're playing with fire." He ran his thumbnail up the sole of my foot, causing me to let out a squeal. He'd just found another place where the nerve endings were connected to my clit. And by the twinkle of his smile, he knew it, too.

One hand grasped my ankle, while the other tortured my sole. I was a panting mess when he let my foot loose. I shoved it quickly back into my boot.

"Let the games begin," he said and raised his glass in a toast. "Just so you know, I always win." He licked his lips like he was savoring something. It was the same way he licked them each time he was between my legs. Like I tasted like honey and sweet cream and he craved me.

So I wouldn't puddle on the floor in a quivering heap, I changed the subject from eating his meat to something a little less titillating.

"Tell me about your ranch."

"Well, to begin with, we didn't get our start on the up and up. My great-grandfather stole some of the finest horses around the country and bred them on his own. McKinley Ranch got its start from thievery."

I let out an exaggerated gasp. "And you judged me."

"Obviously not too harshly since you're sitting here." He topped off our wine glasses and continued. "I'm the oldest son, so I have the responsibility of continuing the family legacy."

"You're going to steal horses? Is that why you were scouting them out at the auction?"

"No, smartass, I was bidding on a few good breeders for the ranch. What were you doing there?"

I knew what he was doing there. "I was doing jailbird stuff. You know, meeting with my parole officer."

"Lucy is your parole officer?"

"Yep, and she noticed you and said you were a stand-up guy."

"That's a lot of pressure."

"I'm sure you can deal with it. She must think highly of you and your family. I don't think she gives out compliments freely. She obviously respects what you've built. How do you deal with all the pressure of running a family business?"

"It's a burden I've learned to live with. My brothers used to think I was the lucky one, but really it was them. They were free to do whatever they wanted. I was raised to be a rancher. I knew exactly where I'd spend the rest of my life."

"Do you think that was a blessing or a curse?" I'd grown up the opposite way. I'd had choices, and then they were taken away. Keanan had never had any choices to take away. I wondered which way was worse: to live a life set out for you, or to set out on a life and never be able to live it.

"It depends on the day. The ranch runs like a finely oiled machine. It's successful, and so we are all successful, but there are trade-offs."

"Like?"

"Like this is the first time I've spent any length of time off the ranch."

"You never go on vacation?"

"Nope. There's no time, and I didn't have any desire to leave."

"Oh, and now you do?"

"That's changed. I came out here for the wedding, and I met you."

"How do I change things?"

"You make me want to leave my ranch. I like being with you as much as I like being there. That's a problem."

"Oh, so now I'm a problem."

He pulled his lower teeth over his upper lip, and I watched the rose-colored skin until it popped free. "You've been a problem since the moment I saw you."

"Was that the moment you accused me of trying to steal Houdini?"

"Who the hell is Houdini?"

The waiter showed up with our salads, and we continued to talk.

"The colt? You know, the one who is a master at escape?"

"You named him Houdini?" He took a bite of his salad and chewed on it along with my name for the horse. "That's perfect for him."

"How is he today?"

"Still trying to get out. He's determined to be somewhere else. Only this time he's tethered to the wall, so he can't get far."

"Poor baby."

"You should come and visit him tomorrow. He likes you."

"I like him, too. He's like a kindred soul."

The ringing of my phone interrupted our conversation. I answered it without seeing who was there. I heard more heavy breathing, and then an edgy voice said, "I won't let you get away." I dropped my phone into my salad.

"What's wrong?"

"Nothing," I said. Keanan was already skittish about my past. I wasn't going to scare him off more because some creepy guy called. "Wrong number."

I wiped the blue cheese dressing from my phone and shoved it into my purse, but I could see by his expression that he wasn't buying the lie I was selling. With a sigh, I admitted, "I lied."

I turned my phone so he could see the call that said *unavailable*. "This is the second call with someone breathing heavy and hanging up. I think Tipsy Ted might have somehow got my number, and it's his way of punishing me for breaking his nose."

"I'll break the bastard's nose a second time if you get another call. The next time it rings, you hand it to me. Okay? And Robyn, don't lie to me. That's the one thing I won't tolerate."

I nodded and let my chin hang to my chest. "I didn't want to chase you away." I raised my eyes to see his expression, and it was soft and full of understanding.

"This isn't your fault. I wouldn't let it scare me away."

The rest of dinner was spent talking about me. I explained how I'd gone to college until the attack. How my parents had disowned me after I went to jail, and how I'd gotten to Mickey's ranch.

"It's been rough for you."

"It's been a journey, all right, but I'm tough. I'm not a quitter."

"That what I like about you. My woman has to be tough. She has to have an exterior made of titanium and a heart made of gold. Ranch life is not easy. It's never done. And there's always some-thing that requires the tenacity of a ring fighter and the patience of a saint."

I wiped my mouth with the napkin and laid it on the table. "I've got the fighter part down."

He placed a pile of twenties next to the check and rose. "Let's go work on the rest."

"How do you propose to do that?"

"I figure if I can get you screaming to God a few times like I did last night, he might offer you some grace."

Chapter 12

I discovered the next morning how much I liked waking up next to Keanan. He was a spooner, and the feel of his arms wrapped around me was a comfort I hadn't known in a long time—if ever. Back in the day, Joe had gripped me like he was holding me hostage. Keanan, meanwhile, held me like he was hugging something cherished. The difference was subtle, but it was there.

I looked over his shoulder to see the time. It was only five-thirty. Next to the clock lay the vibrator. He'd found it in the drawer when he searched for another condom, which we didn't have.

I'd never seen a man so interested in a piece of rubber in my life. He wasn't intimidated by it at all. In all honesty, he had no reason to be. It lacked everything that Keanan had except the part that vibrated like a jackhammer. About halfway through his inspection, he got a bright idea to make up for the orgasms I missed in prison, and since we were out of condoms, that's what he did.

I didn't know a girl could get a friction burn, but by the seventh roof-raising orgasm, I'd had enough. My clit was on fire, and my legs felt like I'd run a marathon.

"Ready for another round?" He was awake and staring as I stared at the rubber cock. "You were in prison for two hundred and sixty weeks. If you had one orgasm a week, and I think that's on the low end, we are still two hundred and fifty-three short of the quota." He reached for the rubber phallus.

"Touch it, mister, and I'll kill you."

Instead, he pulled me close to his body. "Aw, the fighter showed up this morning. I was hoping for the saint."

"You get neither until I get more sleep." I really was exhausted.

He kissed the back of my head. "You get some sleep. I'm going shopping for supplies." He crawled out of bed and left me cocooned in the memory of his warmth and affection. He really was a good man once you got past his hard outer shell. The kind of man who would love the right woman forever. I really wanted to be that woman. I fell back to sleep dreaming of him and was jolted awake by a loud knock on the door.

I pulled the sheet around me and padded to the front door thinking Keanan had locked himself out. "We need to get you a key," I said as I opened the door—not to Keanan, but to Joe.

He walked right in like he owned the place. "A key would be great." He shut the door behind him and pulled me into his arms.

"I needed to see you." His lips crushed into mine. I turned my head, trying to get away from him, but his fingers gripped my hair so tight that tears sprang to my eyes.

My hands clutched the sheet around me. It was either drop the sheet and push him off or maintain my modesty and let him kiss me. I dropped the sheet.

Bad luck knocked at my door again. Just as the sheet dropped, Keanan walked in with a tray of coffees and what I assumed was a bag of condoms.

He looked at me standing naked in the hallway, then looked at Joe. "Who the fuck are you?"

Joe stood back and picked up the sheet, handing it to me as if it were some chivalrous act. "I'm her fiancé. Who the fuck are you?"

Keanan looked at me. He looked at Joe. He looked at the sheet that had fallen to the floor. The light blue of his eyes turned slate gray, and his body became stone stiff.

"I'm no one," Keanan said. He turned and walked out of my cabin.

I wrapped the sheet around me and ran to the porch, but he was already in his truck racing away, so I went back inside to deal with Joe.

"What the hell, Joe?"

"Who the fuck was that guy?"

"He's not your concern." I gripped the sheet tighter around me. "What are you doing here?"

"I needed to see you."

I backed into the living room and pointed to the couch. "Have a seat. I'll be right back."

I turned and ran to my room, where I dressed with haste. When I returned, Joe was pacing in front of the fireplace mantel, murmuring to himself.

"You could have called!" I yelled.

"I did!" he screamed back.

I raced to the kitchen to get my phone and saw there was a missed call from Joe.

"I'm sorry. I was sleeping. I didn't see it." I turned to the coffeemaker and started a cup. "Coffee?"

"No. Who was that guy?"

"He's not your concern." I pulled the creamer out of the refrigerator and splashed some into the cup.

"If he's fucking you, he's my concern."

I yanked the still brewing cup from the pot, splashing the steaming brew on my hand. "Ouch! Shit!" I yelled and headed to the freezer for ice. "I'm not your concern. You're married, for God's sake."

He paced my kitchen and ran his hands through his hair. It was dark like Keanan's, but I no longer had any desire to run my hands through Joe's hair.

I rubbed the ice cube across the burn and watched the red skin turn pink. The ice soothed the burn on my skin, but what was going to cool my temper?

"I can't get you out of my head. I thought you were gone, and then that day I picked you up, I realized we weren't finished. We're not finished, Robyn."

I picked up my phone and walked to the living room. I sent a quick text to Keanan.

Please come back and let me explain.

Joe pulled the phone from my hand and threw it across the room, shattering the glass. "You belong to me. I found you. I saved you. You owe me."

I stepped away from him, trying to gain distance. My initial reaction was fight or flight, but I heard Lucy's voice asking me which girl I was.

I'm the one who's going to defuse this situation and find Keanan and make it all right.

"I don't belong to you, Joe. You got married. You have a child and one on the way. Go back to your wife. I'm not yours anymore."

He bent to the floor and picked up my phone. "You'll never be his. You'll always be mine, Robyn." He tossed my phone on the table, and I could see it still worked, but the glass was cracked like a spider web.

I grabbed it up quickly and walked to the door. "You have to go. Go home to Tanya. Go home to your kid." I opened the door and waited until he walked out. He turned around to say something, but I shook my head and said, "Just go."

I stood on the porch and watched him drive away.

Mickey rounded the corner with a baseball

bat. "Who the hell was that, and what was all that yelling?"

"That was Joe, and he decided to pay me an unexpected visit." I told her the details, and by the end I was sobbing on her shoulder. "Why does everything good in my life have to turn to shit?"

"I'll have Kerrick call his brother and explain things."

She held me for a few minutes and then left me to wallow in self-pity. I texted Keanan at least a dozen more times, but there was no reply, or at least none I could clearly see through the cracked glass.

After an hour of pacing the floor, I felt my time was better spent in manual labor. I found Cole, who happily put me to work mucking out stables. I'd earned myself three good blisters by the time Kerrick came by to see me. His expression was grim.

I tossed the rake against the wall and leaned against the weathered barn wood.

"Did you find him?"

"Yep."

"And?"

"He said it was fun while it lasted, but it's done."

A cry broke from my throat, but I swallowed

it before it could take hold. "He won't even let me explain?"

Kerrick looked at the ground like he was ashamed to say whatever he was going to say. "He's a hard man, Robyn. He has to be. It comes with being the head of the family. He's quick to judge and long to forget."

"So that's it? Some guy from my past shows up without an invitation, and I'm guilty of something?" I remembered the look in Keanan's eyes as he stared at my naked body. I knew he thought Joe and I had done the dirty, but that couldn't have been further from the truth. "Where is he?"

"He packed up and left. He's at some hotel. He won't say where. Give him a day or two. He'll come around. He's just being stupid."

I picked at the blister on my hand until it bled. "I don't have time for stupid."

"He'll come around. The McKinleys are not easy men, but I'm told we're worth it."

"Yeah? Well, I'm worth it, too, and if he wants me back, he's going to have to earn it."

Kerrick gave me a hug. "Thatta girl. You're just like my Mickey. There's a fire inside you, and God help the man who tries to extinguish it."

He stood back and looked at me like he wanted to ask a question.

"What? Just ask."

"Should I be worried about this Joe guy? You want me to run a check on him?"

"No, he's just confused. He has a wife and a kid, and one more on the way. He was living in the past for a second, but I straightened him out." I even risked a smile. "And no blood was shed."

"That's the way we like it." He turned to leave. "Do you want Mickey to come see you?"

I shook my head. "Nope, I'm going to be okay." I would tell myself that lie until I believed it.

Chapter 13

It was a crap night. No sleep and nothing good on television to watch. I finally broke down and bought the damn Wonder Mop on QVC, hoping they would move on to another item if I helped them meet their quota. No such luck.

I balanced my checkbook twice. Cleaned out my already clean refrigerator. Color-coded my clothes and dusted every flat surface in my cabin. By the time the sun rose, I was shaking from the ten cups of coffee I'd had over the past four hours. I pulled on a pair of jeans and the boots Lucy had given me, and I worked my way to the barn, where Houdini was still tethered to the wall.

I knew what he felt like. He was trapped in a

place where he didn't belong; I was trapped here on the ranch until the wedding, and then I'd leave. I could free myself, but I wondered what would happen to the little colt then.

"How's our little escape artist today?" a deep voice asked from behind me.

I whirled around, thinking it was Keanan, but it was Killian. He was the one brother I hadn't really talked to. He didn't seem the talking type. He was quiet and brooding until Megan was around, and then his whole demeanor changed. It was like she lit him up inside.

"I just got here. He seems to be limping around." I looked at the gangly little horse, and my heart lurched.

"It would be best if he stayed off his feet, but he's a busy one. Maybe you could get him to calm down."

"I can try." He *had* lain down and rested his head on my lap on the way back from his last escape, but I'd thought that was because he was plumb tuckered from the trip.

I unlatched the gate and walked in. He hopped around until I got into the corner and slid down the wall to a sitting position on the cleanest bit of hay I could find.

The colt immediately collapsed beside me and laid his head in my lap.

"There you go. He likes you."

"He's about the only one."

Killian grabbed something from the wall and handed it to me. "Try this. Brushing his coat will feel like his mother grooming him."

I took the brush from his hands and began to make long strokes over his soft hair. "Hey boy, when will you learn? These people want to take care of you."

The horse breathed deeply and snorted.

"I know just about everybody here. The girls are awesome; the guys will grow on you. I think you could be happy here if you just gave it a try." I felt like shit giving him advice I wouldn't take myself. Here I was planning my own escape in a few days.

"So since you don't have a mom, I'm going to give you some advice." I listened carefully to the silence in the barn, making sure no one was nearby. "If you meet a pretty filly that turns your head, make sure you don't break her heart. And if she tells you to trust her, you should give her the benefit of the doubt. And if you come into the field and she's naked in front of another horse, don't trot away because she might have a good reason. He could be an old stallion from her past that busted into the field without notice, and she could have been waiting for you. Anyway, just be good to her, because in the end she was probably falling in love with you, and now you've broken her heart."

I heard something shuffle in the barn. I bolted to my feet, upsetting the colt. He whinnied while I looked over the stall to find the barn door swinging back and forth.

Just my damn luck that Killian was there to hear me bleed my emotions all over the neck of a juvenile horse. I went back to the colt, who was struggling to stand, and slid down next to him and nuzzled my head into his neck.

I DIDN'T KNOW how long I'd been in the barn, but at some point I realized there was no light filtering through the windows. Instead of the commotion of horses being moved from their stalls to the field, music from a distance filtered through the split barn wood.

I looked down at the colt, who was no longer sleeping but still in my lap.

"I've got to go, little man." I laid the brush

against his smooth coat and gave him one more gentle grooming before I moved from beneath him.

The poor thing looked up at me like I had some magic potion to make everything all right. I didn't. I could barely figure out my life. I was sadly underqualified to make his life better, but if my presence gave him some comfort, then I'd gladly sit here and hold him. Sometimes all we needed was to be held and know someone cared. I could be that someone for him while I was here.

I opened the barn door to waning daylight and the smell of barbecue. At the main house, people gathered around the porch. Wedding guests were arriving for the upcoming celebration, and judging by the size of the crowd, the entire ranch population was present—everyone but me.

I looked around the parking area. There were three black trucks that looked just like Keanan's. Was one of them his? Big black trucks seemed to be a calling card for cowboys, so I couldn't be sure, but I scanned the crowd and didn't see him.

I knew eventually Mickey would come looking for me, and I didn't want to meet anyone smelling like horse shit and hay, so I hurried to my cabin. Keanan's presence was everywhere.

Sitting on the couch. Leaning against the counter, drinking coffee.

I walked into the bedroom, and his smell was there, too. He was in the sheets. On the mattress. I stripped down and threw my clothes onto the growing pile in the corner, covering up the sundress I'd worn on our date.

I walked into the bathroom and started the shower. Water sluiced over my body, heating and loosening my tense muscles.

Had it only been thirty or so hours since I'd had the best sex of my life and had an ex ruin my future? Since then, I had become the proud owner of a Wonder Mop and made a baby horse think I was his mother.

I turned off the water and climbed out of the shower. I barely had the towel wrapped around my body when I heard my phone ring.

I grabbed it from my jeans pocket on the third ring.

"Hello?"

There was silence, followed by heavy breathing, and then the words, "You won't get away with it."

I fumbled with the phone buttons, trying to disconnect. Once I hit end, I tossed it on my bed.

Who the hell was that?

In record time, I dressed. I approached my phone like it was a poisonous snake ready to strike. The phone felt hot in my hands, but that was my imagination. It was the words that burned: *you won't get away with it.*

I brought up the list of recent calls. Even though my glass was cracked, I could see there were two calls from a number I recognized as Joe's. He didn't leave a message. The third number was blocked.

It had to be Craig Cutter, the asshole in the wheelchair. I knew it in my gut. He was hell-bent on making me pay more. I'd done my time for hurting him. Over eighteen hundred days. Sixty months. Five long years. So, if the blocked number was that asshole who robbed me, he was right; I didn't get away with protecting myself or the martial arts studio. But I wasn't giving him another day of my life. No one would make decisions for me but me. Not Joe, not Craig Cutter, and not Keanan McKinley.

I shoved my phone into my back pocket and walked outside. Hadn't I missed enough? I wasn't missing this party.

"There she is," Mickey said from the front porch.

I spread my arms out wide. "Here I am. Where's the beer?"

Killian reached into the cooler and tossed me a bottle.

Megan put her arm around me and asked, "You okay?"

I unscrewed the cap and sucked down the cold bubbly brew. "I'm perfect."

"Come meet the in-laws."

Megan slid her arm in mine and walked me toward an older man and woman who sat in rockers at the far end on the front porch. A beautiful brunette with eyes like the sky stood behind them.

"This is Kane and Kathryn McKinley, and their daughter, Keara."

"You must be Robyn," Kathryn said.

I gave her a how-did-you-know look. "That's me. It's nice to meet you. You have some really awesome sons." I wrapped my arm around Megan. "If you can get this one down the aisle soon, you'll have a trifecta. Your boys have picked some winners."

Kathryn smiled broadly. "I hear Keanan has taken a liking to you, too."

I drank deep and thought about how to answer her. "Keanan's a good guy, but he's not my type."

Kane sat in silence. I followed Keara's line of sight and saw she'd lasered in on Cole and he was staring back. If those two weren't watched closely, there would be a shotgun wedding happening soon.

Megan walked off to join Killian, which left me alone with the elder McKinleys.

"You say Keanan is not your type. You don't like good looking, successful cowboys?" The grin that lifted the corners of Kathryn's lips was more of a smirk than a smile.

I sat on the top step of the porch and looked up at the woman. "I like them just fine, but I require more than skill in the sack from my man. I require trust. That's not one of Keanan's strengths."

Kathryn roared with laughter. "You're going to be good for him."

"You don't understand, we're not a thing."

"Okay, if you say so. Can you hand me another beer?"

I stood up and walked to the cooler and grabbed two. I'd need another to wash down the sadness of my truth. Keanan and I could have been good together, but I could never be with a man who didn't trust me implicitly.

Once I handed the beer to Kathryn, I walked away toward Natalie. No use wasting Kathryn's time or mine.

"What's up, girl?" Holly said from her comfy chair near the fire. "Where were you?"

I thought back to Houdini and smiled. "I fell asleep in the barn with that poor little lost colt. He seems to have taken a liking to me."

"You're easy to like." She sipped on her bottle of water. "What's going on with you and Keanan?"

"Nothing anymore. We had a few good times, but we're not really suited for each other."

"I don't know, I thought you looked perfect for each other. He may be rigid, but I thought you'd push his boundaries a bit."

"His being rigid wasn't the issue. That part of him I liked. It's all the rest that's in question."

"By the way he looks at you, I'd say there aren't too many questions in his mind."

"You mean 'looked.'"

"No, I mean the way he's looking at you now like you're a tasty T-bone and he hasn't eaten in days."

I followed her line of vision across the fire pit.

Sometime between my arrival and beer number two, Keanan had arrived.

His blue eyes glowed in the firelight, and Holly was right: he looked hungry…or pissed.

"I'm going to head back to the cabin. I'm exhausted."

"I get it. I wanted to sleep for days after I got out of prison. Don't forget, tomorrow night are the bachelor and bachelorette parties at Rick's Roost." She patted her stomach lovingly. "I'm the designated driver for the girls."

"Perfect, I'll be the designated drunk."

I finished off my second beer and tossed the bottle into the nearby trashcan. I said goodnight to everyone I passed and headed back to my cabin. The shuffle of feet sounded behind me, and I knew I wasn't alone.

Chapter 14

I kept walking, even though I knew Keanan was hot on my heels. "You know you shouldn't sneak up on a girl, especially this girl. She's been known to kick some ass and put people in wheelchairs." My no-nonsense voice echoed off the cabins.

"I'm pretty sure I could use an ass-kicking. I'll take my chances." His deep voice practically made the surrounding air vibrate.

Within seconds he was next to me, keeping pace with my almost jog. Of course, for him it was a normal stride. I was winded; he was not.

"What do you want, Keanan?" I stopped at the stairs to my cabin.

"I want to talk."

"The time for talking was when I left you twelve messages."

I stomped up the three steps and opened my door. Over my shoulder, I watched him stop on the bottom step. The look on his face was similar to the colts.

He wanted...no, needed something from me. I was such a sucker for sad eyes.

"I'm sorry about not calling back." He tucked his hands in his pockets and his chin to his chest. "What I need to say to you can't be done through the phone. A man should face his issues head-on."

"I'm your issue?"

He kicked at the dirt under his boots. "No, I'm the issue. You're everything right, and I've done everything wrong." He put his boot on the first step and looked up at me. "Can I come in?"

I looked into my empty cabin, then turned back to him and nodded. "Come on in. I'll make us some coffee."

I left him on the steps and went to the kitchen. I heard the door close, and my heart sped up. My body reacted to his presence like that of a kid who'd just been told they could have their favorite ice cream. Only Keanan wasn't ice cream. He wasn't something you could have once and be satisfied. He was like a rush of adrenaline my body craved.

He stood next to me while I made us coffee. I could smell the spice of his cologne, and it was a delicious mix with the extra bold brew.

When I turned to look at him, his eyes burned hot on my skin. I was dressed in jeans and a plaid button-down shirt, but I felt naked.

When the coffee pot sputtered to a stop, I handed him a cup. I'd had a dozen rounds of sex with him, but I had no idea how he took his coffee.

"Cream? Sugar?"

"No, I like it plain and bitter." He took the cup and brushed my hand in the process. A zing went all the way from my pinky finger to my toes.

"Like your women?" I tossed two spoonfuls of sugar into my mug and turned the coffee white with a splash of milk.

"You're not bitter, and you're far from being plain."

He followed me into the living room, where I sat on a single chair so he couldn't distract me by sitting near me. It was hard enough being in the same room with him. I didn't know how I would hold it together if he sat close enough for our legs to touch.

"I'm bitter about a lot of things. I'm bitter that five years of my life were snapped up because I kicked someone's ass that deserved it. I'm bitter that I'm thirty-two and want children, but I'll have to settle for being an aunt to all those girls' babies." I pointed to the door in the direction of the main house where all my girls were sitting happily with the loves of their lives. "So, you can see, I am bitter."

"I talked to Kerrick. He's supposed to side with the law, but he said you got a bum rap. Said it all boiled down to the fact that you didn't have a mark on you, and the guy was an inch from dead."

I nodded my head because it was true. "I was painted as a badass third-degree black belt—a walking deadly weapon. He was portrayed as an innocent bystander who just happened by." I pulled the coffee to my lips, hoping the sweetness would counteract the sourness I felt in my stomach. "What wasn't elaborated on was the guy was really fucked up on something. He'd just been kicked out of his apartment for violent outbursts, and he was broke. Two of the three were not illegal, but I think the state of someone's sobriety should be considered a factor. People do stupid shit when they're drunk or high."

Keanan raised his hand. "Guilty of drunk stupid shit."

I leaned back and plopped my shoes on the coffee table. "Tell me."

"Which time? I could regale you with stories of drunken disaster. You mustn't forget I'm the oldest of four boys. We were never easy to raise. Hellions, my mom called us." He leaned back and mimicked my body language—feet on the table, coffee in one hand, arms open and lying on the back cushion.

My psych professor would have said his body language was open and honest. I thought he'd look better with me straddling his lap. And that was why I was sitting in this solitary chair with a coffee table between us.

"Make me laugh. I could use a good chuckle."

He laid his head back and stared at the ceiling. "Okay, I've got one." He pulled his feet down and leaned forward. Once he set his coffee mug on the table, he began. "My parents left on a trip and put me in charge. There were to be no parties, no girls over, basically no fun."

"Uh oh, I can already see this is going to end badly."

"Worst whuppin' I ever got. Anyway, we had a tractor, horses, a truck, and an ATV, and us boys got a notion that we should have a party and invite our friends. We bet on which of us would win a race around the property. Add in alcohol and stupidity, and you get a tractor in the river, a truck with a broken suspension, and a horse that's lame because Killian decided to jump the fence and didn't make it."

"What about the ATV?"

"I won. That was the only wise decision I made that day."

"How long before you could sit down without a cushion?"

He put his elbows on his knees and leaned forward. "I got my dad's leather belt for that one, but it didn't hurt as much as their disappointment. They had trusted me, and I let them down. That was my first big lesson in earning trust. You're my first big lesson in giving trust. I'm sorry about yesterday morning, Robyn. I saw you naked in front of another man, and I went back a dozen years. Pulling Ginny out from under some rutting asshole who was getting his payment for a line of cocaine."

The pain on his face was obvious. It was like saying it out loud was reliving the event. His eyes clouded over, and his jaw went slack. His resignation with regard to the situation showed in the downturn of everything from his shoulders to his lips.

"Tell me more about this woman who scarred your heart." I sipped at my coffee and waited. He looked like he was at war within himself. "I won't judge you."

"There's not much to say. She was my high school sweetheart. We went to college, and things went to shit. She wanted new and different. I'm a creature of habit. I want to come home to the woman who loves me every day."

"You were both so young. Did you date anyone else after her?"

He laughs. "Yes, that's all I did was date. I was a one-man dating machine. But dating was it. I guarded my heart like it was a derby-winning horse. No one was getting near it."

It took a lot for Keanan to open up to me. One thing I knew about the McKinleys was that they were all guarded men. They didn't open up easily, and here was this big, brawny man spilling his heart to me now. It touched me and scared me all the same.

"I understand. I felt like whoever my attacker was all those years ago stole something from me. I dropped out of college because I was afraid to walk around campus. Then Joe was there, and he brought me back from near death to life."

At the mention of Joe's name, Keanan stiffened. "Do you love him still?"

I'd had a long time to think about my love for Joe, and it wasn't the kind of love you saw in rom-coms or read about in fairy tales. We weren't volcano hot in bed, but we were comfortable with each other. We could depend on each other—we did—we had to.

"I do love him." It was obvious he misunderstood by the sigh that accompanied his nod. "But I'm not in love with him. It's the kind of love you feel for a childhood friend."

"He's in love with you." He rose from the sofa and walked to the empty fireplace mantel. "It was etched in his face as he looked at your body." Keanan fisted his hands, which caused his knuckles to turn white. "I didn't like the way he looked at you."

"Me either, and he tried to kiss me."

"He what?" Keanan rushed to me and knelt in front of me.

"That's why I was naked. It was either stand there and clutch the sheet or drop it and push him off me. I chose the latter."

He pulled the coffee from my hands and

gripped my palms. His hands were so large that mine looked like a child's in comparison. "I'm so sorry. I left you, and he could have done something to you. I'm a shit of a man, and I don't deserve you, but I want you."

I left my hands in his because it felt nice to touch him. It was a simple thing, but it felt more intimate than the times we'd had sex. Maybe it was because I knew his heart was attached to this action; whereas when we had sex, the only thing that was connected was his dick.

"First, I'm completely capable of taking care of myself. Second, I'm not sure it's me you want. We don't even know each other. I don't know anything about you except that you're good in bed."

"You think I'm good in bed?" He picked up my hands and kissed them both.

"You know you are. My body sings in your hands, but being compatible in bed doesn't mean we're compatible in other areas."

"I think compatible in bed is the biggest hurdle. The rest we can figure out together."

"Why me?"

He leaned back and sat on the edge of the table next to my coffee. "I want what my brothers have. I want a woman to share my life with. I want children."

"You can advertise online, and I'm sure you'd have lots of takers."

His palm brushed over the shadow of his whiskers. "That's not what I want. I want a family, and you're family to those girls, and they're family to my brothers. Kerrick has vetted you, and that's huge. He doesn't trust anyone."

"I heard he ran a security profile on all of us."

"It's his thing. He's hell-bent on protecting Mickey."

"I'm not his issue, but the asshole who keeps calling me from a blocked number might be."

His body grew six inches as he sat up straight. "More calls?"

I pulled my cracked phone from my back pocket and handed it to him. Handing him my phone was an act of trust.

"Look at my recent calls."

His finger scrolled over the screen. He tilted and turned the phone to see past and under the web of broken glass. "Joe, Joe, Joe." He read the missed calls and frowned. "Blocked, blocked. Does the caller say anything?"

"His voice is muffled, like he's covering the phone with his hand, but he says something like, 'You won't get away with it.'"

"Have you told Kerrick?" He handed me back

my phone and placed his warm hands on my knees.

"No, it's not his problem. He's getting married in a couple of days. He doesn't need anything else on his plate."

"You're family. We take care of family." He took his phone from his pocket and typed something on his screen. "Now he knows. He can make a phone call and at least see if the guy is around."

I wanted to argue, but I did feel better knowing someone else knew what was going on. "I met your parents. Your dad is a man of few words, but your mom had plenty. Oh, and watch your sister. I think she has eyes for Cole."

His grew wide at the mention of his sister. "I'll kill him."

"Hey, your sister has something to do with it, too."

"You're right, and she's just like the boys, only she has a vagina."

"That pretty much means Cole is screwed, because a vagina can outthink, outperform, and outsmart a man any day."

"Truer words have never been spoken." He dropped to his knees again and put his head in my lap. I groomed his dark curls the same way I did the colt, slow and soft.

"What am I going to do with you?" God, his hair felt so good in my hands, and his head felt so good in my lap.

"Forgive me, and then if it's in your heart, try to love me."

"Before I can love you, I have to get to know you." I pulled his head up and looked into the most sincere set of blue eyes in my life. "All I know is your body, and I'm not complaining. It's a playground, but we owe it to ourselves to get to know each other."

"You're right. Ask me anything. I'm an open book." He ran his hands up the sides of my thighs, trapping his arms between my legs and the chair. It wasn't a sexual move, but a possessive one.

"Where are you staying?"

"I was in the hotel downtown, but there's a wedding in town, too." He lifted his head and rolled his eyes. "I had a room last night, but tonight I'm in my truck."

I pushed on his shoulders, making him sit upright. "You can't stay in your truck. Why not go back to your cabin?"

"Kerrick gave it to my parents. That way, he

didn't need to be quiet when he and Mickey…you know."

"You're not sleeping in your truck. You can sleep in the spare room here."

"Thank you, but if I'm sleeping here, why can't I sleep with you?"

I thumbed his chin so he was looking at me. "Because we would never sleep." I stood and stepped around him. "I'm making popcorn. Go get your stuff, and we'll watch a movie."

He stood to his full height and width, which was the size of a doorway. "Why don't we make a movie?" He took out his phone and pointed it at me.

"You can sleep in your truck."

"I'll take the spare bed."

Chapter 15

By the time we made it through two *Die Hard* movies, I knew Keanan's favorite color was blue. His favorite food was cheesy grits and hot dogs. He loved dogs but wasn't a fan of cats. He had a business degree. He bred racehorses, which was very different from what they did here. He had a ranch house on the McKinley lands that was as far away from his parents' house as possible. He was wealthy but not arrogant (which I told him was a matter of opinion). He preferred Levi's to any other brand of jeans, and he always wore black cowboy boots.

He learned I had a younger brother with Down syndrome and that my family had moved to Pennsylvania after I'd been imprisoned. I also preferred dogs, but I had never owned one. My favorite color was pink unless it was lipstick, and then I liked a rich berry red. I loved burgers and fries more than almost anything in the world. I had an obsession with Hot Tamale candies. Once I started eating them, I couldn't stop until they were finished. I was low maintenance—a brush of lip gloss and a ponytail, and I was usually ready.

We snuggled on the couch, but he never did anything more intimate than rub my arms and give me a squeeze. By the bulge in his pants that remained half-hard throughout the entire evening, I knew he wanted more, but I was incredibly proud of his self-control. He was proving to me that I was more than sex.

While I brushed my teeth and changed for bed, he grabbed his bag. We played a game of tag with the bathroom. I left as he entered. I lay in bed and listened to the shower run. I imagined his body slicked with water—his skin glistening against the white tile backdrop—his muscles ripped and ready for anything—his hand stroking the length of his amazing cock until he relieved the pressure of his passion.

I groaned and tossed and turned in my bed. Knowing he was in the room next to mine was like being just out of reach of a glass of water after you've run a marathon. It was torture.

I must have fallen asleep because I woke up in the middle of the night with his arms wrapped around my body.

"I'm sorry. I couldn't sleep. Can I stay and hold you?"

How could I say no to that? He wasn't asking me for anything but the comfort of my presence. "Yes, stay with me," I whispered as I turned into his chest and buried my face into him. He smelled so damn good.

I knew exactly how Houdini had felt when he had rested on my lap yesterday afternoon: safe. In Keanan's arms, I felt sheltered, like I'd finally found my way home.

When I woke up the next morning, the sheets beside me were still warm, and so was my heart. He'd done exactly as he promised. He'd spent the entire night holding me, and I'd never slept so well.

"Hey, beautiful." He stood in the doorway, blocking almost all the light, and held two cups of coffee. "You ready to kick-start your day? I found some espresso pods and thought that might give us a boost." He looked so delicious standing there shirtless with his jeans hung low on his hips. That damn V led my eyes straight into his jeans. Keanan didn't say a word, although it was obvious by his rising erection that he felt me eating him up like a chocolate truffle.

I held out my hand and said, "Coffee," like it was a life-saving elixir. And in that moment, it was because without the distraction of freshly brewed coffee, I would have been all over this man. My body was thrumming with arousal. My clit and nipples were vying to see which could swell and harden the most.

He walked to me and placed the steaming mug in my hands. "I thought we could go on a ride today. You do ride, right?"

My mind went straight to *Yes, ride me,* but I knew he was talking about horses. Besides, I'd drawn the line in the sand last night. I was the one who'd said we needed to get to know each other, and he was proving to be a man of his word.

"I haven't ridden in years."

"It's like riding a bike. You'll get back in the saddle, and it will be like no time has passed." He slid into the bed next to me, and I cuddled up next to him with my coffee and a sigh. No morning had been this good in a long time.

An hour later, we were in the stables. He had

Cole saddling up a horse named Honey for me. Keanan was eyeing the back of Cole's head like his eyes were fully loaded .45s and Cole was his target.

Cole made the mistake of saying, "Where's Keara?"

"None of your damn business. You stay away from her." Keanan's voice was like a serrated knife ready to slice a throat.

"Give him a break." I stood on my tiptoes and pressed my lips to the big oafs.

"I'll give him a break. I'll break his nose or worse."

Cole patted the saddle of Honey while Keanan adjusted the saddle of Diesel. "I was just being neighborly," Cole said with no hint of fear in his voice. He was either incredibly brave or incredibly stupid. Just looking at Keanan would tell him he was a man you didn't mess with.

"She isn't your neighbor."

Before I could say another word, my foot was in the stirrup and Keanan's hands were on my ass, giving me a boost into the saddle. They may have lingered there for a second longer than necessary, but I didn't mind. I liked Keanan's hands on my ass.

With a tug of the reins, we were off.

"I don't like him," he said as soon as we were behind the stables.

"You don't like anyone." I flicked the reins so I could catch up with him.

He sidled his horse up next to mine and reached over to touch my arm. "I like you."

"Yes, you do, and I like you. A lot."

It was nice to see his lips turn into a smile. Without those small stolen smiles, he looked like he was grumpy all the time.

We rode to a rocky outcropping at the top of a hill and dismounted. He stood with his front to my back as we stared at the view of Pikes Peak and the Rocky Mountains.

Keanan let the horses nibble at the grass while he nibbled at my neck. "Can I kiss you?" His voice was throaty and needy.

I turned and gripped the collar of his shirt and pulled him down to me. "You better." God, he was an amazing kisser. He explored my mouth like he was searching for treasure. He savored the kiss like I was some sort of delicacy.

When I pulled back, I was breathless and dizzy, and only my head leaning against his chest could stop the world from spinning.

"What we have is special." He stepped back

and placed my hand on his heart. "It beats for you, Robyn."

The rapid rise and fall of his chest were accompanied by the beat that pounded in his chest. My fingertips felt the pulse, and my heart raced to match his. I knew his words to be true. What we had was special. I'd never felt so strongly connected to anyone in my life.

"I know. I feel it, too."

We slid to the ground and kissed like teenagers. My body was tense and tingly. His was hard and rigid all over.

"Let's get you back to the ranch so we can eat and rest. Tonight's going to be a big night for the bride and groom. I see lots of beer and bad choices."

"I choose you."

The words were out before I could think about them. I had no idea what they implied, and I was pretty sure Keanan didn't either, but there was a look of hope in his eyes, and that made the words worth saying.

Back at the ranch, Keanan said he'd take care of my horse while I checked in on the colt. I found him still tethered in his clean stall.

"Hey, little guy, I told you they would be good to you."

I entered the pen and leaned against the rough-hewn wood of the barn wall. Within seconds, he was at my side, rubbing his muzzle against me. He was more like a puppy than a horse. I hoped whoever ended up with this colt treated him well and that he'd find his home among them. It was so important to belong.

"I'm working my issues out with Keanan," I told the horse, who didn't care. All he cared was that I was touching him. "He's not a bad man. He's a good man with a wounded heart. He's more like me than not, and I think maybe we could fill each other's holes." I thought about my words for a second and laughed. "He fills that one fine. What I meant was, I think we can heal each other if we both stop being so stubborn."

"You think so?"

I looked up to see Keanan leaning over the gate.

"You were eavesdropping." My hands came up to my heated cheeks.

"No, I was coming in to see if you wanted to have lunch with me, but if you're more interested in hole filling, I'm game."

I patted the pony on the head and walked to my man. *My man.* It had a nice ring to it. I'd never even considered Joe my man. He was my savior.

He was my friend. He was never what I considered my man, and in that moment I wondered why.

"Can I have both?"

Keanan's brows lifted to disappear beneath a fringe of wavy bangs. "Now darlin', don't go teasing a man with something you don't plan on doing. That's just cruel." He opened the gate for me and pulled me into his arms. "I want you more than anything, Robyn, but you said you wanted our relationship to be about more than sex."

I wrapped my arms around his waist. "I do, but we've shared our favorite colors and foods. Shouldn't there be a balance? I mean…all information and no sex will make Robyn a dull girl."

He grabbed me by my ass and lifted me up. As soon as my legs were wrapped around his waist, he was moving toward the barn door and no doubt my cabin. "We don't want that." Once inside, he took me straight to bed. "Let's satisfy this appetite first, then we'll work on the other."

I fumbled with his belt while he divested me of my clothes within seconds. "You're still over two hundred and fifty orgasms short of the quota." He crossed his arms, gripped the hem of his T-shirt, and tugged it over his head. Looking at this man's chest was like coming upon one of the wonders of the world.

"I'm not going to reach them in one afternoon." My voice was breathless. "Lord knows I'll be happy with one for now. You can help me catch up over time."

He toed off his boots and dropped his jeans. His length pointed right at me like it was saying, *You, I want you.* I wanted him, too.

"I like that." He gripped my hips and pulled me to the edge of the bed. "Mind if I get a little taste?"

He didn't wait for an answer. He covered my sex with his hot, slick mouth and made love to me with his tongue. Just the length of his tongue could rival most men's dicks. He was slow and sensual, then fast and hard. He licked and laved. He swirled his tongue and sucked my clit. When he filled me with two of his fingers, I was gone— over the edge in a quivering, moaning mess.

I barely had a second to recover when he slid his sheathed cock home and stilled inside me. "You like how I fill you, darlin'?" He rocked his hips against me in the most divine way. Talk about a bundle of frayed nerves. "I love being in you. Just you. It's different. It's perfect." He pulled back and thrust forward several times. My heart had crawled into my brain, causing all thoughts to turn to love.

"I love it. I love you. God, how can I love you already?"

He pulled back slowly and slipped back inside me with the same pace. "I'm a McKinley. We aren't easy, but we're worth it." He pulled out and plunged deep. His hands gripped my ass and lifted me—still impaled on his length—and he moved us up the bed. "I want you to love me more than my cock, but loving it is a start."

"I do." I pressed my hand to his heart. "I'm going to heal your heart, Keanan."

"You already have." He slid in and out of me with a steady pace, one that took my buzzing body to new heights. He wasn't hurried, and this wasn't desperate. Today, we weren't trying to scratch an itch or satisfy a need. This was something more. It was an exchange of trust and love.

Chapter 16

We walked into Rick's Roost like we owned the place. At least it appeared that way because the minute we were inside, people parted like we were Moses at the Red Sea.

On one end of the bar were tables decorated with pink balloons, and the opposite had tables with blue balloons. It wasn't customary for the bride and groom to have their parties at the same place, but in this case it worked.

A few minutes later, Keara entered with the men. Being underage and all, she was dubbed the men's designated driver, along with Cole, who didn't look so thrilled. I was pretty sure Keanan had something to do with that. He'd seen the way Cole looked at his sister, and keeping Cole sober was his way of protecting her from too many beers and bad decisions.

Once they entered, Keara came to the girls' side, where she and Holly started with soda while the rest of us tossed back shots of tequila.

"Here's to the fabulous five," Mickey said. "I've never loved a bunch of people as much as I love you. I'm so happy to have you here to be part of my life and my family."

At that, Holly started to cry, because she was all hormones and emotions. But the minute one tear fell, we all started to blubber. It took the burn of another shot to quiet us down.

In the corner of the stage sat a badass-looking man who played the guitar. "Who's the entertainment?" I asked Megan.

"That's a friend of Killian's. His name is Ryker, and he owns a garage in Fury. He was trying to turn it into a bar, but you know, being an ex-con and all, he couldn't get the license. He comes here and plays on occasion when the guys are gathered."

I poured myself a glass of beer from the endless supply of pitchers that made it to the table. "No firearms and no liquor license. Poor guy. Why did he do time?" I glanced across the room and noticed Keanan staring at me. He lifted his glass in a toast, and I did the same.

"Murder." She made it sound like an everyday occurrence, but then again, after you'd spent some time in a cell, you really thought twice about people's crimes. The district attorney had a way of blowing up charges to make sure something would stick. I remember reading through mine and seeing *kidnapping* on the sheet. Turns out the minute you restrain someone it's kidnapping, and since I had pinned Craig Cutter to the ground with my knee, that became a kidnapping charge. It was crazy how screwed up the system was for both the victim and the criminal. I'd been on both sides of the fence, and neither was fun.

"It's funny how you can see a person and not know who they are inside. He doesn't look like a murderer."

It was funny because when you thought about a murderer, you thought about a sinister person with malice in mind. But if I had hit Craig with one more pound of force, I might have found myself in the same position as Ryker.

"He's a good guy with a sad background. He murdered his foster father for abusing his younger brother."

"The guy probably deserved it."

"I think you're right. The courts were lenient, and he only did six years."

I thought about how long five years felt. "That's a lifetime, especially when you're young like him." I watched him pack up his stuff and join the boys for shots of whiskey and beers.

Every once in a while, I'd feel my skin prickle, and each time it did, I knew Keanan was looking at me. One look his way, and my insides started to tingle.

"I see you and my son have made up." Kathryn stood next to me. "He's a good man, Robyn. You could do worse."

What a thing to say. I almost spouted out that I could do better, but I knew that wasn't the case. Keanan was the best. He was a paradox of a man. He was fierce and rigid, yet soft and sensitive.

"He is a good man, Kathryn. You've done right by your boys."

She shook her head. "Raising four boys was tough." She looked over at her boys, then turned her head toward Keara, who sat in the corner of the room with her arms crossed over her chest. "But that one is worse than them all. She'll be the death of me."

"They all make their way."

"That's true, but I have to wonder how many

hearts she'll slay before she gets there. Take the energy and cunning of those four men and pair it with a vagina."

"You sound like Keanan."

"He's chased a bloke or two off the ranch." She nodded her head back to Keara. "That one's trouble with a capital *T*."

"She's beautiful." I looked at the brunette in the corner, and even from here her eyes glowed that same McKinley blue that Keanan's did.

"Kane and I had a good recipe. I'm sure your babies will be beautiful, too." The woman spoke as if my joining the family was a foregone conclusion.

"I'm a little old to be counting on babies. At thirty-two, it isn't a given."

She swiped her hand in that oh-nonsense way. "A fifty-nine-year-old woman in Italy gave birth to twins. Lord, wasn't that silly? She'll be nearing eighty when they are in high school. Imagine chasing a young enamored man off your land at eighty." She gripped her chest like the thought of it gave her pains.

"What do you think of all your boys hooking up with ex-cons?"

She moved around and adjusted her shirt for a bit, as if she were trying on the question for size.

"My boys need strong women. We raised them to be tough men. They aren't easy, and a simpering wife would never do. They need someone who knows what hardship is. Someone with a backbone to stand up for what's right and what's wrong." She glanced over at each of the girls. "Not one of you went to jail for something silly." Her eyes went to Natalie. "Well, maybe that one, but she's not with one of my boys. However, I like her just the same."

"I think we've all grown from the experience. You learn a lot about yourself when you're alone."

"What did you learn about yourself?"

I sipped at the beer and looked over at Keanan. He was playing pool with his brothers, and together they looked so young and carefree.

"I learned I'm made of stronger stuff than I thought. I'm willing to fight for what's important, even though I may end up in jail, and I know I don't want to be alone." As if he felt me thinking about him, he turned toward me and set off in my direction.

With each step toward me, my heart beat harder until Keanan stood in front of me, and it felt like it might burst out of my chest.

"Are you trying to scare her off?" He looked at his mom with a not-so-serious expression.

Kathryn made a *tsk* sound. "Of course not. I'm bribing her to stay onboard. I'm extolling all your virtues. Go away. I haven't been able to tell her about your house."

"I'll tell her about my house. Go pat Holly's stomach and start naming your grandkid. I'm taking my girl dancing." He led me away and to the dance floor, where several people swayed to a country tune talking about love gone right.

"You look beautiful tonight." His hands wrapped around me like I was precious china.

"Not so bad yourself, cowboy." I laid my cheek against his chest and tucked my hands in his back pockets. "I love being in your arms."

We moved around the room in a modified two-step. After all the alcohol and our refusal to let each other go, it was more of a one-step and a stumble. "I love you in my arms. I love you in my heart. I just plain love you." His lips covered mine in a branding kiss. "I know it's soon, but sometimes you just know when something is right. You're everything right."

"How do you know?" I moved close enough to crawl into his body.

"You're a nurturer."

I made the kind of *beep* sound you hear on a

game show when the answer is wrong. "Wrong, I'm a killer, kick-ass woman."

"You're that, too. But you're a good friend and a good person. You took care of every one of those women in prison. They make my brothers happy. You made sure when they got out, each one of them could protect themselves. That was a big undertaking."

"That's just what I do." I slid my hands from his pockets to his chest.

"Yes, it is. You also visit that damn colt every day, and you sit with him so he can rest and heal. You talk to him like he's your child. You're going to be a good mom, Robyn. Our children are going to be blessed."

"Maybe you should sit with your mom and rub Holly's belly."

"How about I lay with you and rub yours and dream about how fucking gorgeous you're going to be when you're big with my child?"

I knew it was the alcohol. "Here you go with your beer and bad choices."

He danced me to the wall and pressed his body against mine. "I didn't get a choice when it came to you. So, there's no way you could be a bad one." Then his lips were on me again, and we stood there against the wall until Killian told us to get a room.

I hung my head in embarrassment and slunk back to the girls. I sat in the corner with Keara while the others got their groove on.

"Have you kissed him?"

Her head snapped in my direction. "Who?" Her voice was the kind that made men fall to their knees. It had that soft throatiness to it that was reminiscent of old-time movies and sex sirens.

"Let's be honest with each other. You're hot for Cole; he's hot for you."

"How can you tell?" She squirmed in her seat.

"It's a gift. Your brother has it, too, so be careful."

She growled and picked up her soda. I knew she'd rather be drinking something stronger, but she was just shy of drinking age. The only reason she was allowed in here was that it was a restaurant and bar; otherwise, she'd be sitting at home in a cabin watching reruns of *Gossip Girl.*

"I've kissed him, but that's it."

"That's enough."

"Says the woman who climbs my brother like a tree." She wasn't being rude. There was a hint of longing in her voice. "Can you imagine trying to date with them around? Add in several dozen ranch hands, and I might as well be heading for the convent."

"There's no rush. You have plenty of time to find the right man."

"How do you know Cole isn't the right one?" She picked up her drink and finished it off with a slurp of her straw.

"I don't know. Only you can know that." I poured another glass of beer.

"How do you know Keanan is right for you?"

I looked across the room and watched him watch me. "Because I feel like my heart will stop beating if he's not around."

A big smile picked up her pout, and I knew she understood what I was saying. I also knew it was going to be a tough road for those two. Not unlike what Keanan and I had to face. Aside from all our emotional issues, we had a geographical barrier I had barely had time to worry about yet —he lived in Wyoming, and a parole officer tied me to Colorado.

Feeling the need for another kiss, I patted Keara on the back in an it-will-be-okay gesture and headed for my man.

I was halfway across the dance floor when another man grabbed my waist and pulled me to him. The poor man never had a chance against the McKinleys. They were like a pack of wolves descending on the guy. Once I was extricated out of his arms and put in Keanan's, the pack, led by Killian, tossed him out of the bar and came back as if nothing was amiss.

Deep inside, I knew I belonged to him, but I never considered myself a part of the larger family until that moment. Each set of eyes was possessive, like I was under their protection. Protecting me was second nature to them. They took care of their own.

Chapter 17

I woke up to a sexy man and a cup of steaming coffee made to perfection with two spoonfuls of sugar and a splash of milk.

"What time is it?"

"Time for you to get up if you don't want to miss the breakfast with the other four."

Whoever decided a friends breakfast was a good idea after a bachelorette party was nuts. I'd have to find out whose brainchild it was and give them a roundhouse kick to the head.

I sat up and stretched and took the coffee. My body ached in all the right places. I had whisker burn between my legs, and my nipples ached from so much action, but I was completely happy knowing I'd spent the night with Keanan. I could get used to waking up to him and coffee every morning.

"What time do you get up at your ranch?" I looked at the nightstand clock that read ten minutes past eight. Next to it sat the vibrator, and a recollection of the number twelve came to mind.

His eyes followed mine to the nightstand. "Generally, I get up at five." He must have seen the question in my eyes. "Yep, we marked off another dozen."

"Holy hell, no wonder I'm sore."

His hand came down to cup my sex. "I can make it feel better."

"I bet you can, but right now all I can handle is this coffee and a shower." He climbed into bed beside me. Keanan didn't look like the kind of man who cuddled, but I'd be darned if he weren't an expert at finding the perfect position to cradle me so I never wanted to leave. "What are you doing today?"

"The boys and I are going to the auction." His body shimmied with excitement. I'd say sex was his favorite pastime, and horses were a close second. He should be a very happy man at this point in his life.

"If you see my parole officer, tell her I've been behaving and I said hello."

He scrunched down to bite my earlobe and said, "I'm going to tell her you've been really bad, but that's really good in my book."

It turned out I did have time for another round. My tender tissue screamed until he seated himself fully inside me, then all that discomfort turned to passion. Minutes later, I was able to mark another orgasm off the list.

Once showered, I kissed Keanan goodbye and headed to see Houdini before I met the girls at Mickey's house. When I arrived, he wasn't in the stall.

"He's in the arena with a few other horses," someone said from behind me.

"Oh." I turned to find Killian grabbing a leather strap from the wall. I'd heard rumors about his dominant personality, but I couldn't see Megan ever bending over for a strap. He followed my eyes to his hand. "It's a horse bridle."

"Of course it is." I didn't know the difference between a rein and a bridle, but I knew one thing: this man made Megan happy, and he brought her out of her shell. Whatever tactic he used was a winner in my book.

"Can I go over and look in on him?"

Killian wasn't the smiling type, but when he did, he lit up the room. "I bet he'd like that." He pointed toward the arena as if the big building weren't obvious.

On my way, I passed the white tent that was now being decorated with pink ribbons. I couldn't believe the wedding was tomorrow. In one more day, there would be another McKinley. A little niggling of envy raced through my veins.

I snuck into the arena and leaned over the rail. My little guy was trotting next to a beautiful white mare. She seemed to be testing his leg out. Then he saw me, and the pretty mare was all but forgotten as he trotted over to the gate.

"Go back and play. I was just checking on you." I stood on the first rail of the fence and leaned over to give him a good pet. He looked over his shoulder like he understood my words, but he didn't budge. Like a puppy, he nudged at my hand until he had it where he wanted it. I scratched his forehead, and I swore his big brown eyes rolled back. "I got to go, but I'll be back. Go and have fun."

I walked to the door, and when I turned around, he was still there by the fence like he was waiting for me. My heart squeezed. If I could have had a horse, this one would have been mine.

We all piled into Holly's SUV and took off to Trudy's Diner. Mickey had been raving about it for years. It wasn't too far away from the supply store, which she insisted we had to stop at to get something she said was a requirement to a happy life.

I was beginning to think the only requirement to a happy life was fresh coffee and a naked man —the rest I could do without. But then I looked at my friends and knew I needed them, too. I couldn't live off coffee and cock for the rest of my life. Although it sounded like something worth trying.

We pulled into Trudy's and piled into a round corner booth. Mickey sat in the center, flanked by Megan and Natalie, and Holly and I sat on both ends. By the amount of food we ordered, you would have thought we were a small army, and in some weird kind of way we were. We were sisters by choice, not by birth. We loved men who were connected as well. It was as if a puzzle had been put together and the final pieces were a perfect fit.

"Oh, before I forget," Mickey said and looked at me, "Kerrick is running a check on Craig Cutter. So far nothing out of the ordinary has turned up, but he's as tenacious as a dog after a bone."

"I don't know who else it could be. The words are a given." I explained to the other girls, who looked like does in headlights, about the calls I'd been getting.

"If it's him," Natalie says, "he'll wish you killed him the first time."

I thought about that for a second. The old me would have fought first and asked questions later. The woman I was now had too much to lose. I had a great man who was crazy about me. My friends surrounded me, and I was going to be an aunt to Holly's baby in a few months. Nope, there wouldn't be any ass-kickings in my future.

The bell over the door rang, and I looked over to see Joe and a young woman whose belly rivaled Holly's. On her hip was a little boy who looked exactly like his father.

Mickey sat up straight. "Isn't that your ex?"

As if summoned, Joe turned in our direction and smiled. He started our way but stopped and pointed to a table nearby where his wife could sit. I watched her follow his directions obediently. I wondered how old she was. She was tiny and frail looking. I'd guess her to be barely drinking age.

Joe walked up and leaned down to kiss me on the cheek. All the girls lifted their eyes in question.

"This is Joe, and that—" I pointed at the

woman in the booth "—is his wife, Tanya, and their son, Joseph Junior."

"I just wanted to say hi since I saw you." He looked around the booth at all the women. "If you have time, I'd love to talk about the other day."

All eyes were on me. "There's nothing to talk about. Have a nice breakfast with your family." He nodded and smiled. He turned slowly, like it pained him to move.

"Oh, honey, you traded up for sure," Natalie said. "He has those beady, untrustworthy eyes, and his wife looks scared to death. Did that ass-hole ever beat you?"

I laughed. Not the giggle kind of laugh, but the big fold-over-your-belly kind of laugh. "Do you think anyone is ever going to be allowed to beat me?" All the girls looked toward Joe and his wife. "He's harmless. In fact, he was my savior when I needed one."

Megan chimed in, "Now you're Keanan's."

I smiled. "Yes, I guess I am. I'm saving him a thousand wrinkles from frowning so much."

We ate everything from waffles to omelets and French fries to ice cream. Holly ate the last two together. Pregnant women always had the weirdest cravings. They also always had the fullest bladders, I remembered, as I got up for my first trip to the bathroom and Holly followed me.

When I came out of my stall, Tanya was standing there.

"Oh, sorry, it's all yours."

She looked toward the door and back to me. "I don't need it. I came in here to talk to you. Joe really wants you to come and stay with us." She brushed a curl from Joseph's forehead. "What I mean is, I'd really like you to come and stay with us. We could be a family together." She gave me a half-hearted smile.

I tilted my head like a confused puppy. "You want me to live with you and Joe?"

She gritted her teeth. "Yes, that's what I want."

I turned on the sink and washed my hands. "I'm not going to do that. I have a boyfriend and a life."

Her expression softened. "Oh, okay."

Holly exited her stall. "She's no freaking sister wife." Holly shook her head like she was trying to get some awful picture out of her brain.

"Tanya, I know Joe is a good guy. He's a savior kind of guy, but I'm not going to come with you. I no longer need saving. You go out there and tell him thanks for the offer, but I'm going to stay put."

She nodded and left.

Holly and I stared at each other in the mirror before we broke out into a laugh. "Holy shit, I think you were going to be the second in his harem."

I let out a ragged breath. "Weird, right?" I wanted to march straight out to Joe and ask him what the hell he was thinking. His wife obviously was not onboard with the little ménage setup he had in mind. Or maybe I was supposed to be the live-in nanny. Either way, it was weird.

Holly and I made it back to the table, and she wasted no time telling the girls about my invitation to be a sister wife.

"Oh, my God, can you imagine sharing a husband?" Megan's eyes grew big and wide.

I turned to look at Joe and Tanya's table, but it was already cleared. They had left in a hurry. "I'm pretty sure he wasn't asking me to be a sister wife. I'm sure he was being nice and offering me another place to stay." I wasn't sure of that at all, but I didn't want the girls to keep talking about it. This particular offer was strange, but it wasn't out of character for Joe to want to help.

Our next stop was the supply store, where Mickey insisted on buying us all horseshoes to hang over our doors. Of course, the open end had to face up; otherwise, our luck would spill out. By the time we got home, we were all full, fat, and happy. I for one was heading to bed for a nap because I knew after the big pre-wedding barbecue tonight, Keanan wasn't going to want to sleep.

How right I was. When he climbed in beside me a few hours later, he made love to me like he'd been gone for weeks rather than hours.

Once we were dressed, he escorted me to where pink tulle ribbons held back the white tent panels and candles flickered on the tables. Red and pink roses decorated every tabletop, and love blossomed in the air.

We sat at two round tables and ate the barbecue Mickey and Kerrick had catered. Beer and conversation flowed freely throughout the night. We all stayed until Kerrick picked up his future bride and carried her to the main house. Couple by couple, we disappeared into our cabins to rest for the full day ahead. There would be no rest in my cabin. Keanan had an insatiable appetite —for me.

Chapter 18

Every hand on the ranch was needed the next morning. If we all pitched in, there would be enough time to get the chores done and the ranch in shape for the afternoon wedding.

I donned my cowboy boots and rattiest jeans and headed to the stables to muck about. Keanan worked at my side. He was comfortable anywhere on a ranch, whether it was sitting high in the saddle or bending low to shovel shit.

"How was the auction?" We hadn't had a chance to discuss it yet. We had more important things to take care of, like our desperate need for each other. Someone was going to have to go on another condom run.

"It was good. Killian purchased another troublemaker—a horse with an attitude. They say he bites, but Killian bites harder, so I'm sure he'll be able to turn the horse around."

"Killian wouldn't really bite a horse, would he?" I tried to picture the large and looming cowboy with his teeth on a horse's ass, but I couldn't.

"No, Killian trains through trust. It's a give and take. The horse has to trust him before it will ever work for him. Kind of like you and me. I have to earn your trust."

"And I have to earn yours." After all, I'd been the one standing naked in front of another person when my partner had come home.

"I trust you, Robyn." He dropped the shovel and palmed my cheek. "I should have stayed to listen, but I'm hardheaded and hardhearted."

I ran my hand down to his package. "And always hard here, too."

"I'm trying to soften up. I really am."

"Don't you dare." I gave him a gentle squeeze. "I like you hard." His dick twitched and hardened in my hand.

"Damn it, woman. How am I supposed to clean out stalls when I can't walk?"

I turned around and started pitching dung into the wheelbarrow. "The faster we get this finished, the faster we can take care of that little problem you have."

He picked up a shovel and tossed pellets over the ground. I'd come behind him in a few minutes and mist them with water, and they would expand into nice, fluffy bedding.

"Now you're calling it little?" He adjusted his pants and went back to work. "What am I going to do with you?"

"Love me."

He leaned against the handle of the shovel and stared at me. "I already do."

My heart tilted and tumbled at his words. Sure, he'd told me he loved me at the bar, but that was after a pitcher of beer and several shots. Things tended to get muddled with alcohol; emotions were often amplified with drink. But this morning, he was as sober as a man on a twelve-step program.

We hadn't discussed the future. I thought we were both afraid of breaking the spell of our current bliss. "When do you go back to Wyoming?" There, it was out there.

"That depends."

"On what?"

We shoveled and misted and moved to the next stall, where it all began again.

"You." We worked well together for a new team. Maybe it was because he'd grown up on a ranch and adapted easily to whatever the task was at hand.

"I thought I'd stay a few extra days if you'd have me."

I dropped my pitchfork and wrapped my arms around him. "I'll keep you for as long as I can have you." The thought of letting him go was painful.

"Now we're talking about my length. You have a real obsession with size." His deep laugh echoed off the stable walls.

"I'll show you size. I'm going to give you a black eye the size of Texas if you don't stop teasing me about the size of your dick." I fisted up and shook it at him.

"There's no teasing, darlin'; only a promise that I'll show you later."

We made it through the twenty stalls of the main stable and moved on to the staff stables. Mickey had expanded those recently, and it took us a few more hours to get them all cleaned out.

Keanan headed over to the barn to help Keagan get a semen sample. They had a new stud and wanted to get a count of his swimmers before they started advertising his bloodline. I made my way to the arena, where I knew Houdini was hanging out with the pretty white horse.

I hoped I could see him before he was put out to pasture. Killian had promised me last night the fence would be reinforced, but he'd also said he didn't think the colt would be running away anymore. When I asked why, he said he'd found a girlfriend.

I'd thought he meant the pretty white filly, but when all eyes turned to me, I knew he'd meant me.

As luck would have it, I missed him in the arena. Tyson was just rounding the corner on a tractor. He was smoothing the dirt for the big event tonight. The catering company was waiting off to the side to bring in the wooden dance floor that fit together in a tongue-and-groove fashion.

Just this morning the place was a fully functioning ranch, and by this afternoon, it had morphed into something that resembled a country club.

Mickey was at a spa day with her future sister-and mother-in-law—a gift from Kerrick to ensure she didn't stress out before the big moment. No one would see her until she mounted her horse and trotted toward her husband. The plan was to get her ready at the spa, and a limousine would deliver her to her horse at the appointed time.

I walked by Cole, who was braiding manes and tails. He had real skill in that department, and I wondered whether he'd be as good at braiding Keara's hair. A man who could do hair was an asset for sure. Mickey's horse, Darcy's Pride, looked like she was ready for a pageant with the wisps of pink ribbon attached to her hair. I could only imagine what the saddle would look like.

Finally, I reached the pasture and climbed over the fence. I looked far and wide over the expanse of land but didn't see the little colt. At first I feared he'd escaped, but one glance at the fence, and I knew that wasn't the case. The spot where he was always stuck had been mended. Killian was a man of his word.

I turned around to leave but got a glimpse of something rushing toward me. Houdini raced in my direction, his bandage gone and his white socks moving in uncoordinated determination. He reminded me of Bambi, all gangly legged and wobbly.

"I told you he had a girlfriend."

I spun around to see Killian. He was on his horse, probably checking the fences.

Houdini skid to a clumsy stop in front of me

and pressed his muzzle into my side. "Why do you think he's so clingy?" I'd never thought to ask about the horse's history, but we all have a history, and it defines who we are and how we behave.

Killian hopped off his horse and pulled Houdini's wounded leg up for inspection. There was a long gash across his knee that was scabbing over.

"He's a rescue. His mom died in childbirth. Another mare cared him for a while, then she abandoned him. Roland brought him here about a month ago."

Knowing he was abandoned just broke my heart. I knew what that felt like. My parents had abandoned me at the first sign of legal trouble. Their excuse had been that they had their hands full with my brother, and they didn't need another albatross hanging from their neck.

"Well, he's in a good place now. He just needs a little reminder that he's loved."

"He seems happier now that he's found you. Sometimes it works that way. You're alone, and then that perfect person walks into your life and changes everything." He mounted his horse again.

"Are you talking about the horse or Megan?" It was obvious he was in love with Megan. He never let her out of his sight. And when they were together hand in hand, they simply glowed with this incredible contentment.

"You decide what works for you. I can already tell you that what you bring works for the colt and my brother."

He trotted off to ride along the fence, and I stayed behind a few more minutes to love on the little horse.

When I made it back to my cabin, Keanan was in the kitchen. He was leaning the horseshoe against the wall above the counter.

"Make sure the open end faces up," I said on my way to the coffee pot. "I don't need any more bad luck, especially when mine is starting to change for the better."

He left the U-shaped piece of metal leaning against the wall. "Upside down doesn't have to be bad luck. My brothers and I used the horseshoe on our house to warn each other."

"Another McKinley secret? Do tell." I put a second cup of coffee on to brew and handed Keanan the first.

"Like many ranches, our family home had a horseshoe hanging above the door, just like you said, with the open end up. So, we decided a long time ago that if there was ever anything amiss, we'd turn it around so it faced upside down.

Anyone entering the house would know something was off. Usually, it was Dad's temper."

"You guys are sneaky."

"We were smart. If you came up to the house and it was turned upside down, you did one of two things: you either braced for trouble or turned and walked away."

I doctored my coffee and leaned against the counter. "So hypothetically, if you came home and found our horseshoe upside down, what would you do?"

He looked me up and down. "Well, that's easy, darlin'. I'd come inside and face my punishment. You'd never leave the horseshoe upside down unless something was wrong. I'd want to right my wrong."

"You don't have to worry, I'd only turn it upside down if something was really wrong. I don't consider arguments to be that wrong because the makeup sex is so right."

"You want to start a fight with me?" He moved in front of me like it was a challenge.

"This day is all about love, and you want to fight?" I traced my fingers down the buttons of his shirt.

"No, I want the makeup sex."

I looked at the clock on the microwave, and

my breath hitched. "Shit, Keanan, look at the time." We were supposed to be dressed and with our horses in an hour. "You'll have to wait." I pushed past him, discarding my clothes as I ran toward the bathroom. I needed a shower before I stood next to my closest friend and watched her pledge her life to another.

Chapter 19

God, was my man hot. Dressed in black jeans and a crisp white shirt, he looked like sex dipped in hot fudge and rolled in sprinkles. Add in the black Stetson and boots, and he was an ad for a magazine—a cowboy porn magazine.

I was dressed in pink, and my hair hung past my shoulders in ringlets. The plan was for girls to ride with their men, and I couldn't wait to sit on Keanan's lap. I wasn't letting him out of my sight all day. There were too many local girls around, and the way they looked at the McKinley men made me want to strip out of that dress and take each one to the mats. A few roundhouse and back-spinning hook kicks could take care of the lot of them.

"Gorgeous." Keanan brushed his lips against my ear. "You're so damn beautiful. I want to eat you up right here." His hands rested on my hips.

Anytime he touched me, my knees weakened. It was a good thing he had a good grip on me because I would have puddled at the toes of his black boots.

"I'll hold you to that after the festivities." I leaned against his back and breathed in the comfort of his scent. It wrapped around me like strong arms.

The *clip-clop* of horse's feet drew my attention. Sitting on a black-as-night stallion was Kerrick. He was dressed like his brother, only he wore a black vest with a pink tie. He rode his horse to the front of the line and turned to wait for Mickey. Cole stood by her horse, holding the reins as the limousine pulled up in front.

First to exit was Kathryn, then Keara. My heart stilled as Mickey emerged, one blinged-out white cowboy boot at a time. Her dress was short in the front and long in the back. It was designed for her ride up the mountain near the cemetery, where she could be married and be near her beloved father. My eyes filled with tears at how beautiful she looked. How happy she seemed. How perfect her wedding was going to be.

Keanan gripped me harder and whispered, "I love you" in my ear. I pinched myself twice just to be sure I wasn't dreaming. The pain told me I was indeed here in the arms of the man I would love forever, watching my friends celebrate their marriage.

Cole helped Mickey onto her horse while Keara spread her dress across its hindquarters. Kathryn handed her the bouquet of pink and white roses, then took her seat in the carriage that would lead us all to the ceremony.

Mickey shook the reins, and her horse walked to where Kerrick stood waiting. His face was one of awe, like he couldn't believe how lucky he was to have found her walking up that dusty road. They waited for the carriage to pass them, then gave us a thumbs up, meaning it was time to ride.

Keanan climbed on first and helped me onto his lap. Keara handed me a bouquet and did the same for Holly, Megan, and Natalie. We followed the bride and groom up the hill to the meadow where they would exchange their vows. Once there, we dismounted and Cole and the other hands took the horses.

In a beautiful meadow below the Rocky Mountains, I watched my friend pledge her undying love to Kerrick. I'd gotten over the idea that he was a cop the first moment I'd seen him look at her. The McKinley men loved deeply, and there was no doubt in my mind Mickey would be well loved and well cared for the rest of her life.

I gripped Keanan's arm and leaned my head on his shoulder as I heard the final *I do*. Holly was crying. Megan was smiling. And Natalie was turning her engagement ring around and around, a reminder that she was next.

"I want that, Robyn. I want my ring on your finger and my babe in your belly."

His voice wasn't loud, but it was heard by more than me. Kathryn didn't miss a thing. She gave me a look that said, *Mothers are always right*, and I said a silent prayer that she was because I wanted the same thing.

After the ceremony, Mickey and Kerrick took a minute to pay their respects at Mickey's father's grave. She laid a special wreath made out of the same roses as her bouquet, and on the satin ribbon it read, *I love you, Daddy.*

We waited for them to mount Kerrick's horse and ride off together to the reception waiting below. This had been one hell of a wedding, and it would be one hell of an afterparty.

By the time the sun went down, the party was in full swing. It was a regular hoedown, with a country band and enough barbecue to feed a small nation. I danced all night with Keanan. For a big man, he was light on his feet.

It seemed like everyone came out of the woodwork for a wedding. I met what seemed like the whole town, from the cashier at the grocer to the lady who'd given Mickey a loan to finance the expansion.

Even Lucy, my parole officer, was present. I was her first case, as she had had to remain a good citizen for ten years before she could be accepted as a parole officer. We were testing each other out.

Keanan must have seen her coming. He told me he'd meet me in the cabin in thirty minutes. His wink told me he had plans for me tonight, and the thrill of anticipation raced up my spine.

"You enjoying the festivities?" Lucy asked me.

"It's really something, isn't it?" I looked around the grounds at all the people. The parking area in front of Mickey's house must have had a hundred black trucks. "How do you know whose truck is whose?"

She reached into her pocket and pulled out her keys. One press on a button, and a black truck about three rows back lit up. "You have to leave long before everyone else. Which was why I was searching for you. I'm out of here."

"It's good to see you again. I've been really thinking about everything you said. I've been living in the present in thirty-two-year-old Robyn's head, and it feels good."

"I'm glad. Looks like you got yourself a fine man." She looked in the direction where Keanan had disappeared into the night.

"I have. You were right. He's not an asshole. He's a McKinley, and there's a difference."

"Glad you recognize it. There's a big difference between men who take what they want and men who earn it."

I nodded my head. She was right. Keanan never took anything I didn't give freely. "I think we have an appointment next week. I'll bring my boots. You get my pitchfork ready."

"That sounds like a plan." We agreed on the day, and she gave me a hug like I mattered to her, and deep inside I knew I was more than a job to her. I suspected she saw her younger self in me.

Once Lucy was safely in her car, I hurried back to the cabin. If I rushed, I could get a candle or two lit before Keanan came home. Tonight was a night for romance.

I raced into the kitchen to grab the lighter,

then dashed to my bedroom, where the candle Mickey had left me still sat unburned.

The wick caught fire and flickered, leaving shadows on the walls, but there was one shadow that didn't make sense. It was the shadow of a man, and I knew without a doubt it wasn't Keanan.

I whipped around to see the dark outline of a man's body in the light of the doorway. This man didn't fill the space like my Keanan. He was long and thin, and I recognized him right away.

"Joe, what are you doing here?"

"I've come to get you."

Fear snaked through me. It slithered up my spine and lodged in my throat. This wasn't the Joe I knew. He didn't enter people's homes un-invited.

I swallowed the lump of terror rising in my throat. "Where are Tanya and Joseph?" Getting him to talk about his family might make him re-alize he'd made another mistake coming here.

"They're waiting for us." He pushed off the wall and picked up a backpack I hadn't seen when I entered. "Let's go." He turned around and ex-pected me to follow, but there was no way.

"I'm not going anywhere with you."

"Yes, you are. There are hundreds of guests

here, Robyn. I'd hate for the wedding to end on a bleak note." Something glinted in his hand. It was a blade that sparkled under the glow of the candlelight.

My initial reaction was to disarm him and call the police, but I didn't want Mickey's beautiful day marred by flashing lights and interrogations, and I didn't want to end up back in trouble with my parole officer, so I played along. "Where are we going?"

"Home, sweetheart, where you belong. Did you think you could get away with this? You belong to me." His words sent chills racing down my spine. They were too similar to the calls I'd received. "Hurry now before that big, stupid cowboy comes looking for you. You'd hate for him to meet the tip of my blade, wouldn't you?"

"They'll all come looking for me." Maybe logic would work. "Taking me won't work."

He laughed, but it wasn't a jovial, happy laugh. It was a maniacal, crazy-person laugh. "I'm not taking you. You're coming of your own free will. It says it right here on the note. I just need you to copy it so it's in your writing."

He walked into the kitchen, and as sick as it made me, I felt I had no choice but to follow: I didn't want to put Keanan in danger. If I removed the threat from the ranch, I could deal with Joe on my own without the risk of anyone getting hurt or Mickey's wedding being ruined.

He handed me a note and a fresh sheet of paper. I leaned on the counter just below the horseshoe and copied it word for word.

Dear Keanan,

The wedding reminded me of how much I missed Joe and what could have been between us. I'm sorry, but I need him. I need to fix what we had.

With affection,

Robyn

There was no way anyone would believe the message, but at least it gained me favor with Joe. I shoved it forward, making sure to hit the horseshoe with my hand and knock it over. When I righted it, I put it upside down and hoped Keanan would get my silent message.

"Let's go," Joe snarled at me.

He swung the backpack over his shoulder and led me out the back door. I looked behind me at the family I'd grown to love and prayed I'd be back soon.

Chapter 20

It was over an hour before Joe stopped the car in front of an old farmhouse. His grandma had lived out in the middle of nowhere, Colorado.

"You'll love it here," he said while he killed the engine. "It's quiet. I can sit on the front porch and see for miles." He opened his door, and under the dome light I could see him smile. Not a welcome smile, but a smile that said, *Do you understand what I'm saying?* Which I did. He was telling me he would see me if I tried to run.

I wondered whether Keanan was already looking for me. Or maybe his old hurts surfaced after he read the note. Did he believe it? I could only hope I'd convinced him of my love for him over the past few days. I'd shown him by sharing my body, my secrets, and my heart. I had nothing left.

I wanted to run, but I'd have to wait for my opportunity. Right now, there was a knife glinting under the moonlight, and when it disappeared, I felt it prick the skin on my back.

What pissed me off the most was that he'd now just ruined my dress. Not only would there be a tear in it, I was sure it would be stained with blood.

"You don't have to threaten me. I came without a fight."

That was a bit of a lie; I'd been fighting with myself the entire way. I wanted to kick his ass, but I also heard Lucy's voice in my head. And I knew if I injured him, it wouldn't go well for me. My mom used to say you could do a hundred wonderful things, but if you capped them off with something bad, then people would only see the bad.

I refused to let my anger influence my future. I knew Joe wouldn't hurt me. He'd been my savior all those years ago. He was just confused, and I was certain I could talk him out of this madness.

Once inside the house, he flicked on the lights. It was late, well after midnight, and I imagined

Tanya and their son were asleep. Not wanting to wake them, I didn't make a fuss.

Joe led me to a room down the long, dark hallway. It was more of a closet than an actual room. *Room* often implied windows and furniture, but all this room had was a rollaway bed and a blanket.

"You're here for the night. It's the timeout room. I figure it's a good place for you to think about what you did to me when you left me."

"I didn't leave you on purpose. I was arrested."

He seemed to contemplate my words. "It's all the same. You were gone." He looked up to the ceiling. "I had to replace you, but now you're back." He shook his head and stomped out of the room, locking the door behind him.

I collapsed on the mattress and pulled the cover over my body. The sting of the cut reminded me there was no gain without pain. I'd endure whatever I had to in order to get back to Keanan.

Above me, I heard the creak of a mattress, then the whine of a woman, and I knew it was Tanya. "I'm tired," she cried.

"Show me how much you love me." Joe was making her suffer for me, and I felt the bile rise in my throat. I remember the days he climbed between my legs late at night and demanded the same words of love. I'd always thought it was sweet the way he needed my love, but now I wasn't sure. "Tell me, Robyn."

My heart stopped. I stared up at the ceiling and prayed she didn't correct him. I'd never known him to be a violent man, but I also hadn't known him to be a kidnapper either. He was obviously capable of anything.

The hairs stood up on my arms when I heard the headboard slam against the wall and her scream, "I love you." I closed my eyes and thought about Keanan and how many times he'd told me he loved me. I wanted to hear him say it again and again.

Sometime in the night, I drifted off to sleep. When I woke a few hours later, the door to the closet was open and a backpack sat on the edge of the bed. I rummaged through it and found some of my clothes.

It didn't take me long to change into the jeans, T-shirt, and tennis shoes Joe had stolen from my cabin. I stuck my head out the door and looked both ways. Up ahead, I heard the clang of dishes, and I went in search of the sound.

Sitting down in front of Joseph was Tanya, feeding him scrambled eggs and bacon. She looked up at me. There was no hate in her eyes; just regret.

"I didn't choose to come here." I wanted her to know it wasn't my desire to ruin her life with Joe.

"We all have choices." She looked at her son, and I knew she stayed because of him.

I glanced around the room, looking for Joe. "Where is he?"

Her eyes skirted the room, then settled on the kitchen window, where the sun was just beginning to rise. "He's outside in the barn, collecting eggs."

"Will he be long?"

She shook her head and looked toward a foil-wrapped plate on the counter. "I saved you breakfast. You should eat."

I grabbed the plate and ate the eggs, bacon, and toast she had set aside for me. "Thank you." I was hungry. It had been just a few hours since I arrived, but adrenaline had a way of firing up an appetite, and I knew I'd need energy to work my way out of this situation.

"You're welcome," she said in a sweet young voice.

One thing that had bothered me since I'd seen her the first time was her age. She looked so young and innocent. "How old are you?"

"I'm twenty-two." She looked down at the plain gold band that decorated her finger.

"How did you and Joe meet?"

She looked at her son, then down at her pregnant belly. "He saved me."

My world turned dark and dim. "What do you mean, he saved you?" I gripped the table, afraid I'd fall from my seat if I didn't steady myself, because I knew in my gut what her next words were going to be.

"I was attacked at college and left for dead. He found me, and he saved me."

The eggs came up before I could stop them. I raced to the sink, where I lost my breakfast. "Where were you?"

She sipped her tea and let out a deep breath. "I don't like to talk about it."

I ran the water and washed the bitter taste from my lips. "I have to know."

She pulled up her shirt and showed me a large scar across her left ribs. The same mark I sported on mine. The slash of a right-handed man who attacked from behind.

"I never saw him coming," she said. "I was walking out of the library and turned down the sidewalk. I felt the cut first, then there was nothing. Whoever did this hit me over the head, and I was out. When I came to, Joe was there with the police."

I started to heave again. I thought back to his visits at the prison. He'd told me he was going back to school so we could have a better future when I got out, but he'd actually gone back to school to collect another girl. Somehow this seemed like my fault, like if somehow I had stayed out of prison, this girl wouldn't have been his second victim.

I raised my shirt and showed her my scar. "He saved me, too." I said the words with fierce accusation.

Tanya stared at my scar and then choked on her tears. "Oh, my God."

"You have to be calm. He can't know that we know." I rushed to her and pulled her shirt over her burgeoning belly, then swiped at the tears running down her face. "I'm going to get us out of here."

Tanya's face turned white. "I hated you." She dropped her hands into her palms. "Every time he made love to me, he said your name, and I hated you for it."

I gripped her shoulders and pulled her toward me. "If we're being honest, I hated you because you were living my life. You were married to Joe, and you had a kid. Has it been awful?" I felt a mix of emotions from rage to sadness.

She pulled back and shook her head. "No, he's possessive and demanding, but the only time he hit me was when I told him I wasn't you." She rubbed her cheek like she felt the sting all over. "I've never done that again. Once I got pregnant the first time, he calmed down a lot. He knew I wasn't ever going to leave him. How could I? I'm uneducated and a mother." She took the towel she had on the table and wiped at Joseph's mouth. "When we moved out here into the country, it got better. He kept telling me I can't get myself into trouble out here, but I think he was talking to you."

"I'm sure of it." There was no doubt he was referring to me getting arrested. In hindsight, I could see how Joe had orchestrated our lives. I'd tried to go back to school, but he'd kept reminding me of the attack. Eventually, I believed him when he told me I'd never feel safe there, so I quit. "You know you and your kids aren't safe with him, right?" I had to know she was onboard with leaving because I would never leave her behind. I felt responsible for her being here.

"I know. I've known that for some time now. As soon as you got out of jail, he was obsessive

again, but not about me. He followed you everywhere. He was in a rage when you told him to
come home to me. We followed you to that diner,
and he threatened to take my children if I didn't
persuade you to come home with us."

"Did he hurt you?" I'd seen her face when she
left the bathroom. It was a mixture of relief and
dread. And now I understood why she'd felt that
way: relief for me that I'd said no, and dread
knowing he would be disappointed in her.

"No, he told me I was useless, but I'm used to
hearing that. I was never you. I was a poor sub-
stitution."

Joseph banged on his tray, and Tanya pulled
him out of the high chair.

I held out my arms and asked, "Can I hold
him?"

She handed him over to me and walked to the
sink to start the dishes. He had her trained well.
Joe never liked a mess, and yet he'd made a big
one out of so many lives—mine, Tanya's, Keagan's, my now estranged parents', even Craig
Cutter's...the list could go on. But I needed to
focus on my plan.

I held the boy on my hip and bounced him.
"Whatever happens today, just follow along,
okay?"

She gave me a weak nod.

When boots pounded on the back porch, both of our gazes swung to the door.

"Trust me," I whispered just as Joe entered.

He saw me with Joseph on my hip, and his eyes softened. "That's a beautiful sight. Soon I'll have my son in your belly, too." He walked over and kissed both Tanya and me on the cheek. He acted like walking toward his two wives was an everyday occurrence.

Tanya continued to wash the pans, but her hands shook. I reached out and rubbed her shoulder. I knew I needed to get her away from Joe. She was going to break any second now, and that wouldn't be good for any of us.

"Tanya isn't feeling well. She was going to take Joseph and lie down. Weren't you?" I gave her a play-along look.

"Yes," she said. She dried her hands and reached for the baby, but Joe grabbed him first.

"I got him. If you're sick, I don't want you infecting my son. His other mother can tend to him."

I could hardly breathe. I was out of my element here. There were too many variables. Too many risks. I could definitely incapacitate Joe, but I wouldn't put Tanya or Joseph at risk, just like I couldn't put anyone from the wedding party at risk last night. I had to come up with a plan.

The only plan I could formulate was sex. Joe was like any other man, and the mention of sex would change his mind about having Joseph with us.

"Joe," I said in a come-hither tone. "I was hoping to spend some time alone. It's been so long."

He looked at me with skepticism. "What are you up to?"

I was about to blow it by trying to act like someone I wasn't, so I let the Robyn of old out. "I'm trying to get you to fuck me since you've been fucking that whore for years. Now if you'd just give her back her brat, we can get on with our shit." That was the Robyn he visited in prison. The one who was angry at the world. The one he recognized.

He looked toward Tanya. "Get into the timeout room now!" he yelled. He stalked after her, handed her a crying Joseph, and locked her in the tiny room.

"I want the key," I said and held out my hand. "I don't want your soft heart feeling sorry for her and letting her out before we're through." What I meant was, *I don't want her out because I plan to beat*

the living shit out of you and leave you for dead, but
instead I smiled and waited for the key, and the
idiot handed it to me. I tucked it into my pocket
and led him away from the room.

"Don't be pulling any of your martial arts shit
on me," he warned.

I walked in front of him into the living room.
"You used to love my martial arts shit." I spun
around and kicked his feet from beneath him and
straddled his hips. He was faster. He had that
blade out and at my neck, poking through my
skin.

I didn't flinch. I played along. "You used to
love it when I took you down so I could go down
on you." I backed away from the knife and
grabbed at his belt. A drop of blood ran down my
chest from the small puncture wound he gave me.

He looked at my hand on his buckle. "Now
we're talking."

I swiped at the blood on my chest and wiped
it across his lips. "Do you like it when I bleed?"

He flicked out his tongue and tasted my blood.
My stomach lurched, and I wanted to vomit all
over him. I'd been suffering without even
knowing it for a decade.

I reached down and pulled my shirt over my
head. His eyes went straight to the scar he left on

me and then raised to my breasts. Breasts he had no business looking at.

"Like what you see?"

His right hand still gripped the knife, but it was no longer at my throat. Instead, it lay beside his head, just waiting to strike.

His left hand rose and traced over the scar on my ribs. "I saved you, and you owe me your life."

I grabbed his wrist and pressed it to my breast. I needed him to have a moment where he wasn't thinking.

"Yes, you saved me." I leaned over and brushed my lips against his. I nearly threw up in his mouth, but I had to stay in control because not only did I have to save myself, I also had to save Tanya and Joseph. One mistake, and we were all in serious trouble.

When his dick became hard beneath me, I knew I had won. Wars had been lost because a man thought with his dick rather than his mind, and this was war. One he would lose.

I ground against his hardness until he moaned and his fingers loosened around the knife. It fell from his hand. He went to grab for it, but I pressed my breasts into his face and he lost track of what he was doing.

When the lace of my bra rubbed over his lip, I

had him where I wanted him. In one move, I had him turned over with his hands behind his back.

"You fucking bitch," he screamed while he fought against my hold. The more he fought, the more pressure I put on his bent wrists until one snapped. I was sure the sound could be heard through the house.

"I hear you like it rough." I squeezed both of his wrists under my hand and listened to him scream while I grabbed the knife. "I hear you like knives, too." I pressed it to the base of his skull. All I needed to do was push, and he'd be gone for good.

"Baby, you don't want to go back to jail. Who do think they're going to believe? You—a convicted felon—or me?" He began to fight, but I twisted his broken wrist and made him scream out in pain again.

We were at an impasse, and all I could do was keep him here until someone showed up. I knew if I let up on him, he'd retaliate, and I'd end up like I had when all of this started. I'd be lying on the floor within an inch of death waiting for my savior, and it wouldn't be Joe.

In the distance, I heard sirens, and I prayed like a disciple it was Keanan. I started chanting, "Please be him. Please be him."

The sirens wailed, and I kept up the chant until the door busted in and the police surrounded us.

"Drop the knife!" the police officer yelled, and I did. I raised my hands and climbed off Joe. When I turned around, I saw Kerrick and Keanan. Their eyes held a thousand emotions, but one of them was love.

"Thank God," Joe said. He stumbled to his feet, holding his wrist. "She broke in here last night and locked up my wife and kid in the closet down the hall. She's obsessed with me, but I've moved on." God, he was a good actor, but he'd had to be to get two women to fall for him like we did. "Seriously, check her pocket. She's got the key to where my wife and son are locked up."

I remained with my arms in the air while the officer put his hand into my pocket and pulled out the key. He handed it to another officer while Joe told him where to find his poor wife.

I knew from experience to say nothing, but I stared at Keanan and hoped he'd see through Joe's lies.

The officer returned with Tanya and Joseph. Joe began act two. "Oh, thank God you're safe." He made a move toward his wife and son, but the officer told him to stay put. "Tell them, honey.

Tell them how she broke in and terrorized us all night."

The look on Tanya's face was one of confusion. She wanted to believe the lie, and for a second I thought she might corroborate his tale, but her eyes went straight to my scar and she shook her head.

"It's a lie. Everything he said is a lie. He kidnapped her. He brought her here and held her in that room for hours. She locked me in there to protect me and *my* son." She emphasized the word *my* and pulled Joseph close to her chest.

Once the truth was out, Joe turned to tears and begging. He was put into handcuffs and led outside, and I was fully clothed and in Keanan's arms. I was home.

Chapter 21

Kerrick drove while Keanan held me in his lap. We were breaking the law by not wearing seat belts, but we needed to be in each other's arms. If I could have crawled into his body, I would have.

"I didn't leave you. I mean, I left you to protect you. He threatened me by threatening people at the wedding."

His hands ran over my drooping curls. "I know, darlin'."

"I was so worried you'd believe the note."

"I trust you." His lips brushed across my tear-stained cheeks. His fingers touched the Band-Aid Kerrick put on my neck after he cleaned my wound. "I found the note, but more importantly, I saw the horseshoe. It was like flying the American flag upside down. It was a sign of distress. I raced to our room and saw the candle burning. What woman leaving her man would light a candle first? Not my woman."

I turned in Keanan's lap and faced Kerrick. "Oh, God, the wedding. You're supposed to be at home, making love to your wife."

"I have the rest of my life to make love to my wife. I had only a few hours to find you."

"How did you find me?"

"He basically left us a map. First, you said you were going to Joe's. Second, he showed up at breakfast, which Mickey found odd, so she told me." Keanan gripped my hip, and I knew he was unhappy about my omission of that fact. "Third, there were the calls Keanan told me about. I dug deeper and found out Joe was the blocked caller. Then it was a matter of tracking him to his grandmother's house."

I laid my head against Keanan's broad chest, and for the first time since I'd left the wedding, I relaxed.

I was jarred awake when the truck left the smooth pavement and turned onto the dirt road that led to the ranch. I rubbed my eyes and watched as my home came into view. It was an odd feeling to think of this as home because I wasn't attached to the ranch at all. I was attached to the people.

As we approached the main house, everyone ran outside to greet me.

Mickey pulled me from the truck seat and wrapped her arms around me. After she squeezed me for minutes, I was passed from person to person like a cheerleader on prom night. They all hugged me and kissed me and told me how worried they were. At the end of the line was my Keanan, waiting to take me home. Anywhere he was would always be home.

We stayed in bed for two days, making both love and promises to each other. On the third day, I stood on the front porch of my cabin and waved goodbye to him. Not a forever goodbye, but an until-I-can-straighten-my-shit-out-and-get-to-you goodbye. He had a ranch to run, and I had some unfinished business.

I borrowed a truck and drove out to Joe's house to pick up Tanya and Joseph. They needed a second chance, too, and there was no better place to get one than the ranch.

We had to stop by the district attorney's office and file the report that accused Joe of attacking us when we were young college students. It was taxing for Tanya because her life had taken a sharp left when she thought she was going right, and I felt sort of responsible for it all.

On our way to the ranch, I took them for hamburgers and fries. Nothing soothed heartache better than grease and chocolate shakes, which we ordered and devoured.

"What am I going to do now?" She handed Joseph a stray fry and patted her full belly. "How am I supposed to support two kids by myself?"

I didn't know the answer, but I knew she'd find resources at the ranch. "It will all come together." For some reason, I was sure of that.

When we got to the ranch, Mickey had a cabin ready. The girls had rushed around and found a crib for Joseph. The refrigerator was full, and the closet had hand-me-downs from Holly. Once Tanya assured me she'd be fine, I left her in her new home to get accustomed to her new life and went in search of Houdini. The colt was my one happy place besides Keanan.

When I got to his enclosure, he wasn't there. I raced outside and found Cole shutting the gate to a horse trailer. "Where is he?" I demanded.

Cole gave me a strange look. "He's going to a new home."

I dropped to my knees and cried. It was too much to have Keanan and Houdini leave on the same day. Cole wrapped his arm around me and gave me a brotherly hug.

"Get your hands off my woman."

My head snapped up to see Keanan almost running to me. Cole staggered back and took off toward the barn.

"I thought you left?!" I swiped at my tears and rushed to meet him halfway.

"I did, and I got halfway to Wyoming when I realized I won't get a damn thing done without you by my side. I need you, Robyn. I need you next to me always. How do you feel about living in Wyoming with me and your colt?"

My colt? That meant he was taking Houdini. I leaned forward and kissed him. "Do you think I can work it out with my parole officer?"

He cupped my cheek like he did when he had something important to say. "It's done. I stopped by Lucy's on the way back. There was no way I was coming back here and not picking you up."

"I can go?" I hopped up and down and clapped my hands.

"Yes, with a few stipulations." He picked me up and started toward my cabin.

"What?"

"I have to breed her a winner. You have to have weekly phone calls with her until she can get you transferred to a local parole officer. You have to name our first child Lucy."

"I'm not naming my son Lucy."

"Darlin', if it means I can drive you off this ranch in twenty-six minutes, I'll name him anything she wants." He picked up the pace until he was running.

"Why twenty-six minutes?"

He busted through the door and went straight to the bedroom.

"I have one minute to strip you naked, five minutes to make you scream my name, fifteen minutes to pack whatever you're taking to Wyoming, and five minutes to convince you to stop at City Hall and marry my sorry ass."

I tore at my clothes until I was naked. "What if you make me scream your name twice? I can come back for whatever I want later, and you can rush me to City Hall because I'd marry you in a second."

He dropped his pants and climbed between my legs. "You just saved us at least ten minutes."

I pulled him down on top of me. "Use that time wisely."

For the first time he entered me bare, and I didn't care because it was my hope that soon I'd be able to give him a son named Lucy.

Chapter 22

ONE YEAR LATER

A row of black trucks made their way up the driveway to our Wyoming house. It was like the cowboy mafia had descended on us.

I held little Lucy in my arms as her aunts and uncles pulled up in front of our home. This was her first family reunion. She was a classic McKinley, with her dark curls and sky blue eyes. Her dad looked down at her with pride. He beamed like a hundred-watt light bulb every time he saw her.

Mickey waddled toward us on the arm of her husband, Kerrick. She was expecting twin boys in two months, and she was huge.

Holly stepped out of her truck with baby

Grace in her arms. She was a beauty with the McKinley blue eyes and her mother's blonde hair.

Megan and Killian exited the next truck; there were no babies in their near future. They were having way too much fun practicing.

Tanya, Joseph, and little Robyn—the daughter she named after me—got out of the fourth truck with Tyson, who was wrapped around the family like they were his prizes.

In the distance, a few more trucks appeared. One belonged to Natalie and Roland. She was just starting to show, and pregnancy looked good on her. The last truck to show up was Cole's, and when he stepped out with Keara, I knew things were about to get exciting.

I touched my husband's arm and whispered, "Let's have a beer and visit with family before you shoot him."

He relaxed under my touch. "I'll give him twenty-six minutes." He smiled and greeted our guests.

I snuggled up next to him. "Why twenty-six minutes?"

"I like that number. A lot can be accomplished in twenty-six minutes."

The memory of our last day at Second Chance

Ranch brought a smile to my face. I still wasn't a fan of even numbers, but I did love that one.

I said a silent prayer that Cole could win my husband over in that amount of time. If not, I hoped he was fast because he'd need twenty minutes just to clear the McKinley lands.

Sneak Peek into
Redeeming Ryker
RYKER - TWENTY YEARS AGO

Raptor Savage didn't put up with losers. He didn't put up with laziness, and he didn't put up with liars. Today, I was all three.

The sunbaked asphalt pulled at my sneakers. The trees whispered, *'Turn around, run for your life.'* Each inchworm step I took closer to home slapped my backpack against my butt, but that was nothing compared to the ass-whoopin' I'd get from Dad today.

My report on Abraham Lincoln had been due today, the same report I'd told my mom I'd finished, which meant I was a liar. I hadn't done the stupid report. Hiding out in the shop and listening to the War Birds talk strategy was more fun than writing about a dead president. That made me a lazy loser. I'd gotten a big, fat zero for my grade.

Dad would shout, *The report is important, school and getting educated is the only job you have.* And I'd roll my eyes or shake my head or just let my shoulders slump. Abraham Lincoln couldn't teach me a thing. He was dead.

Ask me to write about the gun that killed him, and I would have brought home an easy A. Guns, I knew.

I snaked through the bikes lined up like dominoes in the gravel parking lot as my backpack slipped from my shoulders.

So many bikes at the club meant trouble. Dad was busy, so maybe I wouldn't get a butt blistering after all.

As the president of the War Birds MC, this was Dad's world, and Mom said he ran it like he was God.

God made the laws. He made the rules. He handed down the punishments. Raptor Savage could make people shake in their sneakers with the lift of an eyebrow. I got that look a lot.

Mom always said my spirited nature would serve me well when I grew up and took over the club. Dad always put an "if" before that statement. "If he grows up."

I stepped back from the door and slipped around the side of the building. Mom was out back with my brothers, Silas and Decker. Next to them was that pesky little girl, Sparrow. She always looked up at me like I was a movie star.

"Glad you're home, sweetie." Mom never called me sweetie in front of anyone else, because that would make me seem like a sissy, but I liked when she said it. "Today's Dad's big meeting, so I need you to hang out here with the kids. I have to get inside and serve beer."

I looked around the parking lot at the motorcycles I didn't recognize. "Who's here?"

"Friends of your father's. It has nothing to do with you."

I glared at the kids playing in the dirt. "That's not true." My voice didn't sound like eight-year-old me. It sounded more like six-year-old Silas when Mom told him to take a bath. "I have to babysit, and that means it has everything to do with me." I hated babysitting. Silas was fine. At six, he took care of himself. But Decker was just a baby, which meant diapers, and then there was Sparrow. She stuck to me like gum on a shoe.

I threw my backpack toward the stairs. It skidded across the gravel and clunked to a stop against the bottom step. "Is this about Goose?"

Goose was a War Bird who'd been killed last week after a cop stopped him for speeding. I didn't understand it—Goose was a good guy.

Mom looked over her shoulder toward the club entrance. "Not now, Ryker."

Uh oh. She'd called me Ryker, which meant she was losing her patience. I looked toward the kids and let out a long breath. "Okay, but is this about the cop who shot Goose?" Officer Stuart had said Goose pulled a gun first, but that had to be a big, fat lie. Goose would never shoot the police. Dad's words replayed through my head: *'That cop has been targeting motorcycle gangs. His goal is to clean up Fury.'* Fury was a small dot in the mountains. The entire town couldn't fill up the high school sports stadium. How much cleaning up did we need?

"Dad invited the Rebels over to discuss the growing tension in the area. He needs to get it under control before more people get hurt. I need you to help me out." Mom put her fingers under my chin and closed my open mouth. "Take good care of them." She didn't wait but walked into the club. The club that would someday be mine.

"Hi, Hawk." Using my nickname, Sparrow pulled on my hand. Her fingers were pink and sticky. "Want some candy?" She reached into the

228

pocket of her dress and pulled out a piece of lint-covered licorice.

"Gross." I yanked the candy from her little fist and tossed it toward the parking lot. "It's dirty."

"It's mine." She took off toward the candy that lay in the dirt.

With two giant steps, I grabbed her around her waist, swiping her off the ground.

The rumble of motorcycle engines stopped me like I'd walked into a brick wall. Pulling in front of the club were at least ten more Rebels. "Too many."

I raced back to the playpen where Decker slept. Silas drew in the dirt with a stick, and I dropped Sparrow to her sandaled feet.

"Silas, watch them for a minute." I'd never seen the Rebels up close, and I didn't want to miss my chance.

He looked up at me with Dad's eyes. Steel, gray eyes that said it all even before the words came out. "You're supposed to stay with us."

Sparrow stomped her little feet, causing the soles of her shoes to light up. "Yeah." She looked up at me with the crazy cool eyes only she had. "You're supposed to sit with me." Her one blue and one brown eye begged me to stay.

"I'll be right back. Stay here." I crept to the

corner of the club and wiggled the loose board just enough to slip inside the storage room. The place smelled like leather and sweat and anger, but I tiptoed forward and slid behind the stack of crates. I pressed my ear to the crack between the boxes.

Dad's voice was loud and clear and calm. He talked about rival gangs, feuds, the sheriff, and what they were going to do.

I peeked over the crate of brake pads and counted the heads I didn't recognize. There were twenty-five Rebels in our nest. This was epic. Never had there been so many enemies in one place without someone needing a doctor.

Something creaked behind me, and I swung around.

Sparrow squeezed through the hole. *Little brat.* "What are you doing?" I whispered. "Go back," I gritted my teeth.

"No." She said, a little too loud.

I slapped my hand over her mouth. "Shh. This is a secret." I pulled her close. "You can stay if you can be quiet."

She nodded, and I went back to my hiding place. She tucked up next to me, and we listened. Or, really, I listened while she peeled the stickers from the boxes in front of us. At least she was being quiet.

All the War Birds were there. Well, all but Goose. Kite, Dad's vice president, screamed about being targeted. Some of the members paced the room. They reminded me of the time I cornered a stray cat in the garage. Its hair stood on its back while its tail twitched from side to side.

I'd once heard someone say, *'The tension was so thick, you could cut it with a knife.'* I never understood what that meant until now. The air was thick like Mom's pudding, and it was hard to breathe.

"Your problems aren't my problems." The rebel leader leaned back and crossed his hulk-sized arms over his chest.

"It won't be long before it spreads to your club." Dad leaned forward with his elbows on his knees. "Can't we have a truce between the two clubs until the problem with the police is under control? We don't need to be fighting wars from every side."

Mom crossed in front of me with a full tray of bottled beer. I ducked lower so she wouldn't see me. Sparrow's mom, Finch, followed behind, picking up the empties. I didn't know her real name. No one went by their real name at the club.

We were War Birds with names like Hawk, Raptor, Kite, and Vulture. The women always chose stupid sissy birds like Warble, Robin, or Sparrow. I looked down at the little bird next to me. She wasn't so bad. She was like me—spirited.

The front door burst open, and a pair of cops filled the doorway.

Dad jumped from his seat. "This is a private meeting," he pointed to the door, "and private property."

The big cop, the ugly one, put his hand on the butt of his gun. "Just here to keep the peace." There was something creepy about his voice. Something dangerous about the way his fingers scratched against the gun.

"Only peace here." Dad spread his arms wide enough to stretch open his leather jacket and show off his War Bird belt buckle. The belt usually held his gun, but he carried no weapon today. He was in a room of enemies—unprotected. Or so it seemed. I knew Dad, and he no doubt had a plan.

Mom popped the tops off two beers and handed them to the cops.

To my surprise, they took them. I guess they didn't have to obey the rules. They were cops.

Finch passed in front of us, and Sparrow

sprang to her feet. I knew she would bolt toward her mother, so I picked her up and tossed her backward toward the broken panel. She stumbled against one box, knocking it down. The loud bang shattered the silence.

Everything changed in an instant. Guns drew and shots fired—lots of shots. Bullets flew through the air with the hiss of a mosquito, only a thousand times louder. Metal hit metal with the ding of a pinball machine. Wood splintered from the rafters above.

People fell to the ground in front of me. Sparrow screamed, and I grabbed her, crouching with her behind the brake boxes, and I prayed we wouldn't be next. Prayed until my mom crumpled to the ground. "Mom." Still holding Sparrow, I sprung from my hiding place and ran to where she lay in a pool of blood.

"Where are your brothers?" Her words, no more than a whisper, were hard to hear with the popping sounds filling the air. I crushed Sparrow beneath me and hugged the cement floor.

"Outside. They're safe outside." I reached for Mom, trying to find her wound.

Sparrow popped her head from under me and screamed.

Mom's eyes grew wide. "Get her out. Save her.

Save your brothers." Her words slipped slow and wet from her lips. "Promise."

The wooden beams splintered, sending chunks of wood flying through the air. Clouds of white chalk burst from the walls.

My heart exploded in my chest, and tears ran down my cheeks. "Mommy."

Her head fell to the side.

"Mommy." I was a man but cried like a child. "Don't leave me." I turned her face toward mine and wiped the blood that trickled from her mouth. "I promise."

Her once bright blue eyes faded to the color of cold, gray concrete.

Bullets buzzed. People collapsed. Sparrow screamed and screamed and screamed.

I swept her into my arms and ran toward the door, but hot fire shot through my shoulder. I stumbled. I fell. Blood covered the walls, the floor, the bodies.

I scrambled to stand, but my sneakers slid on the smooth concrete. I slipped and fell over and over again until I couldn't move. I couldn't breathe. I was going to die.

Sparrow lay beside me, but she was quiet. Dead quiet. Blood seeped across her yellow dress like spilled ink on paper. The bright sunflower pattern disappeared in the crimson pool.

I'd failed. I'd failed Sparrow. I'd failed my brothers. I'd failed to keep my mom's final wish. "I promise I'll never fail anyone again," I cried. Everything turned to black.

Get a free book.

Go to www.authorkellycollins.com

About the Author

International bestselling author of more than thirty novels, Kelly Collins writes with the intention of keeping the love alive. Always a romantic, she blends real-life events with her vivid imagination to create characters and stories that lovers of contemporary romance, new adult, and romantic suspense will return to again and again.

For More Information
www.authorkellycollins.com
kelly@authorkellycollins.com

Acknowledgments

I want to thank you, the reader, who have traveled this journey with me. I write for you, and I'm grateful you read my words.

I'll miss the McKinley's, but don't count them out. I may decide to visit them in Wyoming in the future.

Hugs,
Kel

Made in the USA
Las Vegas, NV
12 April 2021